NEW YORK REVIEW BOOKS
CLASSICS

ON THE MARBLE CLIFFS

ERNST JÜNGER (1895–1998), the son of a chemist and pharmacist, was born in Heidelberg and early on developed a fascination with war and soldiers. As a teenager, he ran away to join the French Foreign Legion, then enlisted in the German army on the first day of World War I. Jünger's first book, *Storm of Steel*, provides a graphic account of his experiences. While he kept his distance from the Nazis, he was firmly right-wing and expressed his anti-Marxist ideas for a postcapitalist, utopian society in a series of treatises that culminated with *The Worker: Dominion and Form* (1932). In 1939, while living in Überlingen near the Swiss border, he began to write *On the Marble Cliffs*, which was published later that year, initially escaping censorship because of Hitler's admiration for Jünger's earlier work. After the war, Jünger went on to compose several more works of speculative fiction and nonfiction, including *The Glass Bees* (1957), also published by NYRB Classics, a novel about a future tyrannized by technology. One of the most controversial of twentieth-century German writers, Jünger was the recipient of numerous literary prizes and continued to write until his death at the age of 102.

TESS LEWIS is a translator from French and German. Her translations include works by Peter Handke, Philippe Jaccottet, and Christine Angot, and a collection of essays by Walter Benjamin for NYRB classics. She is a 2015 Guggenheim Fellow and a 2022 Berlin Prize Fellow at the American Academy in Berlin.

JESSI JEZEWSKA STEVENS is the author of the novels *The Exhibition of Persephone Q* and *The Visitors*. Her work has appeared in *The New York Times*, *The New Yorker*, *Foreign Policy*, *The Paris Review*, and elsewhere.

MAURICE BLANCHOT (1907–2003) was a French writer and philosopher whose books, including *Death Sentence*, *Thomas the Obscure*, and *The Space of Literature*, frequently blended narrative and theory. After editing the *Journal des Débats* from 1932 to 1940, he continued to contribute book reviews to the magazine once it became pro-Vichy. Among these was his review of *On the Marble Cliffs*, which displeased the censors.

ON THE MARBLE CLIFFS

ERNST JÜNGER

Translated from the German by
TESS LEWIS

Introduction by
JESSI JEZEWSKA STEVENS

Afterword by
MAURICE BLANCHOT

NEW YORK REVIEW BOOKS

New York

THIS IS A NEW YORK REVIEW BOOK
PUBLISHED BY THE NEW YORK REVIEW OF BOOKS
435 Hudson Street, New York, NY 10014
www.nyrb.com

The translation of this work was supported by a grant from the Goethe-Institut.

First published as a New York Review Books Classic in 2023.
Originally published in the German langauge as *Auf den Marmorklippen*.
The afterword by Maurice Blanchot originally appeared in *Faux Pas* by Maurice
Blanchot, translated by Charlotte Mandell, ISBN 9780804729345, pp 252–256.
It appears here by permission of Stanford University Press.

Library of Congress Cataloging-in-Publication Data
Names: Jünger, Ernst, 1895–1998, author. | Lewis, Tess, translator.
Title: On the marble cliffs / by Ernst Jünger; translated Tess Lewis.
Other titles: Auf den Marmorklippen. English
Description: New York: New York Review Books, [2022] | Series: New York
    Review Books classics
Identifiers: LCCN 2022010898 (print) | LCCN 2022010899 (ebook) |
    ISBN 9781681376257 (paperback) | ISBN 9781681376264 (ebook)
Subjects: LCGFT: Novellas.
Classification: LCC PT2619.U43 A913 2022 (print) | LCC PT2619.U43 (ebook) |
    DDC 833/.912—dc23/eng/20220304
LC record available at https://lccn.loc.gov/2022010898
LC ebook record available at https://lccn.loc.gov/2022010899

ISBN 978-1-68137-625-7
Available as an electronic book; ISBN 978-1-68137-626-4

Printed in the United States of America on acid-free paper.
10 9 8 7 6 5 4 3 2 1

CONTENTS

INTRODUCTION

I.

SOME PEOPLE live more history than others: Born in Heidelberg in 1895, the German literary giant Ernst Jünger survived a stint in the French Foreign Legion, the rise of the Third Reich, two World Wars, fourteen flesh wounds, the death of his son (executed by the SS), the Partition of Germany, and Reunification before his death at the remarkable age of a hundred and two. Perhaps no historical rupture had a greater influence on his thinking, however, than the rise of industrialized warfare across both World Wars. A soldier as much as a writer, Jünger memorably declared in his diaries in 1943 that "Ancient chivalry is dead; wars are waged by technicians." Articulating the consequences of this transformation became the central obsession of his work.

Jünger's fascination with the ways in which technologically driven projections of power would reshape traditional civilian life and geopolitics have secured his legacy as an unignorable diagnostician of the modern epoch. He is today to industrialized warfare what his contemporaries Walter Benjamin or Siegfried Kracauer were to the rise of mass-produced culture: All three drew connections between technology's assault on the inner life of the individual and fascism's weaponization of the mob. Yet while Kracauer and Benjamin, prominent voices of the Weimar socialist left, denounced fascism from the start, Jünger was very much a man of the right. Though he continues to be widely read, his significant literary achievements can be contemplated only with ambivalence. He remains one of Germany's most celebrated and controversial writers—by far the most interesting to have ever emerged from the interwar right.

2.

The book you are holding in your hands, the most famous of Jünger's novels, was published in Nazi Germany in 1939 and censored by the Gestapo in 1942. It was thanks to Hitler's admiration of Jünger's earlier work that *On the Marble Cliffs* was published at all. When other party officials pushed for its immediate suppression ("He has gone too far!"), the Führer reportedly replied: "Leave Jünger be!"

It's not hard to see why the novel attracted the attention of the censors: *On the Marble Cliffs* charts the slow infiltration and eventual destruction of a sophisticated, Elysian society by a barbaric forest tribe whose ruthless leader sows anarchy and terror. Set, like all fables, in a distant time of its own, the story centers on two battle-hardened brothers who've renounced war, politics, and worldly concerns for a monkish existence as botanists. They live apart from the simmering chaos, high up on the Marble Cliffs.

The novel was immediately received as an allegory for the rise of the Third Reich, but as Jünger points out in a postscript included here, "People understood, even in occupied France, that 'this shoe fit several feet.'" In other words, what happened in Germany wasn't historically unique. Echoes were soon to be found in Axis Italy, Vichy France, and the Soviet Union, not to mention in the nascent authoritarianism stirring within Western democracies today. As Jünger saw it, Hitler's nihilism was part of a more general crisis threatening modern civilization.

Whatever the politics of the book—and they are nothing if not equivocal (Jünger claimed elsewhere that the novel was "above all that")—there's no denying its icy polish. The novel is defined by its fantastical Mediterranean landscape, and we spend much of our time admiring the view. To one side of the cliffs lies the Marina with its lush vineyards and islands that "float on the blue tides like bright flower petals"; to the other, the Campagna, populated by rough but noble cattle herders, and bordered by the "dark fringe" of the forest, where the forces of anarchy lie in wait. There is much to lose: jeweled lizards, red vipers slithering as if in a single "glowing web," astonishing orchids, magical mirrors, abundant vineyards, rarified libraries. This symbology flickers throughout the novel like reflections on a lake, captivating yet shifting, and ultimately eluding fixed interpretation. The imaginary world is at once classical and modern; perhaps this ancient-seeming realm isn't quite so distant as we thought. There are both automobiles and ballads dedicated to a "gluttonous Hercules," shotguns as well as Roman stone.

The most striking quality of *On the Marble Cliffs* is to me its stillness. If fiction is the art of lending time to concepts and truths that seem to exist *outside* of time, *On the Marble Cliffs* aims for just the opposite. It is an exercise in "draining time," to borrow the phrase the brothers use to describe the study of botany. Until the frenzy of the final battle scene, the book distills itself to a single, suspended moment. The narration hovers over the landscape like a charge in the air. It's the quiet before the storm, or, in our botanists' case, before they "fall into the abyss."

Throughout his oeuvre, Jünger remained preoccupied with this idea of stopping time. One of the few hopeful symbols to appear in the novel is the mythical mirror of Nigromontanus, designed to concentrate sunlight into a magical flame that transforms all it devours into an "imperishable" state, a process of "pure distillation" that takes place beyond the reach of either the narrative or the historical durée. One can imagine that Jünger—who after the Second World War experimented with LSD—viewed *On the Marble Cliffs* as just such a temporal transcendence, a way of preserving those values that Nazism perverted: chivalry, dignity, knowledge, beauty. It is not a protest novel but, like the mirror of Nigromontanus, a kind of "security in the void."

3.

This framing of *On the Marble Cliffs*—the author's own— complicates the invitation by Jünger's hagiographers to read it as political critique, thereby exonerating him of his own far-right leanings. I tend to agree with Jünger that *On the Marble Cliffs* is not merely an allegory for the rise of the Third Reich. In fact, it's difficult to extract a sustained political allegory from any of his works.

Jünger's politics were complicated, if not incoherent. A decorated veteran of the First World War (he made his literary debut with a bellicose, best-selling diary from the trenches,

Storm of Steel) who was praised by Hitler but who refused to join the Nazi Party; a self-taught conservative intellectual (Jünger never completed university) who won the admiration of Marxist writers like Bertolt Brecht; an incurable elitist sympathetic to communist centralization (he opposed liberalism above all)—the Weimar-era Jünger projected an aloof, aestheticizing, and ultimately paradoxical strain of fascism. Kracauer captured what feels most damning about Jünger's political thinking during this time in a review of his controversial treatise *The Worker* (1932) for the *Frankfurter Zeitung*, in which he accused Jünger of having "metaphysicized" (*metaphysiziert*) politics: What about real, tangible action in our own historical moment? Metaphysics is an escape.

These ideological contradictions—or is it political ambivalence?—extended throughout the Second World War. The tendency to view the world through the metaphysical lens of cycles of power as opposed to "right and left" certainly seems to have granted Jünger, then an influential conservative voice, a great deal of moral latitude in distancing himself from the horrors emerging around him. Ever aristocratic, his critiques of Hitler could appear to be as rooted in intellectual snobbery as in moral outrage. He once complained that the Nazis "lacked metaphysics." They waged war like technicians.

Jünger spent the Second World War as a military censor in Nazi-occupied Paris, where he kept up his ironical circle of acquaintances. His closest companions during this time included the prominent legal scholar Carl Schmitt, a racist and an early supporter of the Nazi Party. Then again, his diaries reveal him to be just as close to the conspirators behind the von Stauffenberg plot on Hitler's life in 1944. Jünger himself was investigated, but no concrete evidence could be found tying him to the attempted assassination; the main conspirators were executed. There is no doubt he considered Hitler a vulgar yet ultimately indomitable monster. The sheer, nihilistic scale of the genocide in Nazi concentration and POW camps crystallized his despair as well as his conviction that more active resistance was pointless. "I am overcome by a loathing for the uniforms, the epaulettes, the medals, the weapons, all the glamour I have loved so much," he confessed during a brief tour of the eastern front. There's a reason a quip by Jean Cocteau (not exactly exemplary in his own wartime behavior) regarding Jünger's conduct during these years endures: "Some people had dirty hands, some people had clean hands, but Jünger had no hands."

What did it really mean to be hands-on at such a time, when protest often amounted to nothing more than self-sacrifice? It isn't a question I like to ask. Jünger's son, briefly imprisoned for dissent, was later declared killed in action in Italy, though the two bullet holes found at the base of his skull suggested an execution by the SS.

The veterans and botanists in *On the Marble Cliffs*—much like Jünger himself, who studied zoology and spent long afternoons in occupied Paris collecting beetles—also delay intervention until it is too late. They are elegists more than dissidents, hunting for rare orchids as the Head Forester's campaign advances on the classical civilization below. Yet the novel contains enough recognizable allusions to the Third Reich that it no doubt took courage to publish it. A torture hut where the Head Forester's enemies are flayed is modeled on Hitler's concentration camps for political and social deviants, the first of which were established in 1933; Jünger is likely to have seen prisoners marched past his temporary residence in Lower Saxony. It has been noted that the Head Forester bears a resemblance to Hermann Göring, the notorious commander in chief of the Luftwaffe and himself an avid hunter. Nazism, furthermore, valorized forests and their connection to the German Romantic spirit. The novel's highs come by way of Jünger's gift for the chilling aphorism. Of the character Braquemart, modeled on the Nazi propaganda minister Joseph Goebbels: "He was of that breed of men who dream concretely, a very dangerous sort." Its lows follow slips into dour, elitist didacticism: "When the sense of justice and tradition wanes and when terror clouds the mind, then the strength of the man in the street soon runs dry... This is why noble blood is granted preeminence in all peoples."

To my reading, *On the Marble Cliffs* is a daring but ultimately inward-looking achievement. It is as if Jünger built himself an ivory tower in which to wait out Germany's darkest decades. He never left. Nor did he repent. Until his death, Jünger dismissed criticisms of his wartime behavior. As he aged, he appealed to the growing asymmetry between himself and his younger critics: You weren't there.

On the Marble Cliffs serves as a key to the cosmology Jünger developed in these later years. All the major motifs of this novel—serpents, language, nihilism, chivalry, dreams, Spenglerian theories of history as cyclical—return throughout his major wartime and immediate postwar works, most notably *The War Diaries* and the techno-dystopia of *The Glass Bees*. In the most generous light, they present an argument for the preservation of beauty, refinement, and human dignity in the face of Armageddon; in the harshest, a justification for a retreat into aesthetics and abstraction in the face of all too real atrocities. I recommend reading *On the*

Marble Cliffs at different times of day, with both approaches in mind.

Tess Lewis's new translation makes this double reading possible. This edition does the crucial work of reinstating the novel's intended fabular atmosphere, muted in previous iterations and yet so essential for understanding a man who thought in images over concepts, and who warned against the enormous dangers of "dreaming concretely." The rhythmic prose captures the nostalgia, the suspension, the "presentiment of doom." For the first time in English, *On the Marble Cliffs* lets its eerie, "rich red lining" show.

4.

In Paris, where Jünger often discussed politics with the women who frequented his intellectual circles, he was struck in 1942 by his own observation that "women are becoming more intelligent." The line has stuck with me. It recalls the gendered nature of war and the codes of chivalry in which soldiers like Jünger were steeped. It complements his declaration that ancient chivalry—a torch historically carried by men—is dead. It hints, in the end, at a profound crisis of faith: The pursuits and traditions that Jünger believed gave life its meaning were rendered not only anachronistic but impotent in the face of pure "connoisseurs of power."

The murmurs from the wings of 2022 tell us that democracy hasn't been this weak since the Weimar years and that populism is on the rise. The consensus explanation is that the twentieth century's refutation—and rectification—of preexisting hierarchies has left many, and above all men, unmoored. These voters, the thinking goes, are newly susceptible to the dark charisma of today's Head Foresters.

A letter to the editor published in *Der Spiegel* in 1982, written in response to one of Jünger's final public interviews, offers a heedful addendum to this kind of political pathologizing. The author of the letter was a local representative of the Bundesland of Niedersachsen, and the translation is mine: "In certain academic circles, it is often discussed to what extent simpleminded workers are made receptive to totalitarian movements. All too often, this discussion overlooks the extent to which these same self-appointed elites distance themselves from basic democratic values." *On the Marble Cliffs* at once evidences and invites its own critique: An enduring sense of nobility, stripped of a politics, sets its own traps.

My fear, these days, is that it's the populists who are becoming more intelligent.

—Jessi Jezewska Stevens
May 2022

ON THE MARBLE CLIFFS

I.

You all know the fierce melancholy that overcomes us at the memory of happy times. How irrevocably these have fled, and we find ourselves separated from them by something even more pitiless than vast distances. In the afterglow, too, these images appear even more enticing; we think of them as we do of a dead lover's body, buried deep in the ground, now appearing before us like a mirage, and we tremble at its greater, more spiritual splendor. Again and again, in our parched dreams we grope for every detail, every lineament of the past. And we feel we have not been allotted our full share of life and love, yet no amount of regret can bring back what we have lost. Oh, if only this emotion could serve as a lesson for every moment of happiness we do enjoy!

And the memory of our years under sun and moon become sweeter still when fear has put an abrupt end to them. Only then do we recognize how fortunate we humans are to live from day to day in our small communities, under peaceful roofs, engaged in pleasant conversation, and with affectionate greetings morning and night. Alas, we always recognize too late that these simple things offered us a cornucopia of riches.

So it is that I, too, look back on the years we lived on the

Grand Marina—only in memory are their charms revealed. To be sure, at the time it seemed that many a problem and care clouded our days and above all that we needed be on guard against the Head Forester. That is why we lived with a certain austerity and dressed simply even though bound by no vow. Twice a year, however, we let our garments' rich red lining show—once in spring and once in autumn.

In the fall, we drank as wisemen do and paid honor to the exquisite wines that thrive on the south-facing slopes of the Grand Marina. When, in the vineyards, we heard the winegrowers' laughing cries amid the scarlet foliage and dark clusters of grapes, when, in the small cities and towns, the winepresses began to creak and the smell of fresh pomace drew its heady veil over the farms, we would descend and join the innkeepers, coopers, and vintners to drink with them from the rounded jug. There we would always find jovial companions, for the country is a rich and beautiful one where carefree leisure abounds and wit and high spirits are the coin of the realm.

Thus, evening after evening we sat down to festive meals. During these weeks hooded watchers patrolled the vineyards from daybreak to nightfall, armed with rattles and shotguns to keep the gluttonous birds in check. They returned late with garlands of quail, of speckled thrushes and figeaters, and their booty soon appeared on the table in bowls adorned with grape leaves. We also enjoyed roast chestnuts and fresh nuts with the new wine and above all the superb mushrooms they hunt for with dogs in local forests—white truffles, delicate morels, and red Caesar's mushrooms.

As long as the wine was honey-colored and sweet, harmony reigned over the table and we would sit in peaceful conversation, often with an arm draped over a neighbor's shoulder.

But as soon as the wine began to have an effect, releasing its coarser elements, our vital spirits were roused lustily. This gave rise to brilliant duels decided by the weapon of laughter, the jousters distinguishing themselves through the facility and candor with which they wielded ideas, a mastery honed only in a long life of leisure.

More than these fleeting hours of sparkling wit, however, we treasured in the depths of intoxication the silent walk home through gardens and fields even as the morning dew began to form on the ruddy leaves. Leaving the small town through the Cock Gate, we would see the lakeshore aglow on our right, while to our left towered the Marble Cliffs burnished with moonlight. Between them stretched the vine-covered hills into which the path disappeared.

Bound to these walks are memories of a radiant, astonished waking that filled us with both awe and exhilaration. We felt as if we had emerged to the surface of life from its depths. Like a knock that rouses us from sleep, an image would pierce the darkness of our rapture—perhaps the horn of a goat such as peasants in these parts mount on tall poles in their gardens, perhaps an eagle owl with yellow eyes perched on the roof ridge of a barn, or a meteor speeding and crackling across the firmament. Each and every time we would stop short as if petrified, a sudden shudder running down our spines. Then it seemed we had been granted a new faculty with which to see this land; we looked through eyes endowed with the power to see the gold and crystals in gleaming veins far beneath the glassy earth. And then, gray and shadowy, they would approach us, the ancient, indigenous spirits of this land, resident here long before any cloister bells rang or any plow carved a furrow. They hesitantly drew near, their coarse, wooden features bearing an inscrutable expression mingling terror and joy; and we gazed on them, our hearts at once alarmed and deeply moved. At times they seemed to want to speak but soon they dispersed like smoke.

We would cover the short remaining stretch to our Rue-Herb Retreat in silence. When the light flared in the library, we would look at each other and I would see Brother Otho's face shining with sublime radiance. In this mirror, I recognized that the encounter had been no illusion. We shook hands without a word and I climbed to the herbarium. Nor did we ever discuss such experiences at a later date. Upstairs, I would sit for a long time at the window in high spirits and in my heart I could feel existence itself unspooling its golden threads from the spindle. Then the sun rose over Alta Plana and illuminated the lands up to the border of Burgundian territory. The wild escarpments and glaciers sparkled white and red and the reflection of the high banks trembled in the Marina's glaucous mirror.

On the pointed gables, the redstarts now began their day and fed their second brood, whose hungry chirps sounded like the whetting of knives. Rows of ducks ascended in flight from the lake's reed belt, and in the gardens finches and goldfinches picked the last grapes from the vines. Then I would hear the library door open as Brother Otho stepped into the garden to check on the lilies.

2.

But when spring arrived, we caroused like fools—as is the local custom. We wrapped ourselves in motley garb with fabric patchwork bright as plumage and donned stiff, beaked masks. Then, cutting foolish capers and waving our arms like wings, we skipped down to the small town where a tall Fools' Tree had been erected in the market square. There, in flickering torchlight, the masked procession started out, the men parading as birds and women costumed in magnificent gowns from olden days. They called out playful taunts, their high voices mimicking the tinkling of music boxes, and we answered them with shrill bird cries.

From the taverns and the coopers' workshops the marches of the feathered guilds beckoned—the goldfinches' thin, piercing warble, the barn owls' whirring zither, the wood grouses' humming double bass, and the squeaky hand-organ with which the hoopoe fraternity accompany their scandalous verses. Brother Otho and I joined the black woodpeckers, who beat their marches with cooking spoons on wooden tubs and held council in a fools' court. Here drinking took skill, for we had to sip our wine from the glass with straws stuck through the nostrils of our beaks. When our heads began to spin, a few turns in the gardens and moats along the town wall refreshed us; we also fanned out over the dance floors or took off our masks under the pergola of an inn and dined in the company of a fleeting love on escargots à la Bourguignonne served in pitted pans.

On those nights, the shrill bird cries rang out from every corner until dawn—in dark alleys and along the Grand Marina, throughout the vineyards and chestnut groves, from the gondolas adorned with lanterns floating on the dark expanse of the lake, and even among the cemeteries' tall cypresses. And always, like an echo, came startled, fugitive cries in response. The women of this land are beautiful and brimming with that generous vitality old Petardier calls bountiful virtue.

As you know, it is not the sorrows of this life but rather the times of exuberance and wild abundance that bring tears to our eyes when we think back on them. So does, deep in my mind's ear, this play of voices lie, especially that stifled cry with which Lauretta met me at the town wall. Although a white, gold-bordered hoop skirt hid her limbs and a mother-of-pearl mask covered her face, I immediately recognized her in the dark alley by the way her hips swayed with each step, and I slyly hid behind a tree. Then I startled her with my woodpecker laugh and pursued her, flapping my wide, black sleeves. On the hillside above, where the Roman stone stands in the vineyards, I caught the exhausted woman and pressed her, trembling, tightly in my arms, my fire-red mask bent over her face. When I felt her limp in my grasp, as if dreaming and spellbound by some enchantment, I took pity on her and with a smile raised the bird mask to my forehead.

Then she too began to smile and softly put her hand on my lips—so softly that in the silence I heard only the sound of my breath wafting through her fingers.

3.

Otherwise, day in, day out, we lived in great seclusion in our Rue-Herb Retreat. This hermitage stood on the edge of the Marble Cliffs, in the middle of one of those islands of rock one sees protruding from the vineyards here and there. The garden was cultivated in narrow beds won from the rock, and along the loose rock walls that edged these beds sprouted an abundance of the wild plants that flourish in fertile vineyard earth. And thus early in the spring blue pearl clusters of the grape hyacinth bloomed and in the fall we delighted in the winter cherries, their fruits gleaming like red lanterns. But in all seasons the house and garden were bordered by silvery green rue bushes, from which a muddled, swirling scent rose when the sun was high.

At midday, when the searing heat cooked the grapes, the hermitage stayed refreshingly cool, for not only were the floors tiled with mosaics in the southern style, but also many of its rooms were recessed deep into the cliff. Still, at this time of day I enjoyed stretching out on the terrace and listening, half asleep, to the cicadas' crystalline song. Then swallowtail butterflies forayed into the garden and settled on the saucer-shaped flowers of Queen Anne's lace and the jeweled lizards crawled out onto the sun-warmed rocks of the cliffs. Finally, when the white sand of the serpents' path blazed like a furnace, the lancehead vipers slid slowly onto it and soon bedecked it like hieroglyphs on a scroll.

We had no fear of these creatures, which lived in great numbers in the nooks and crannies around the hermitage; rather, we were enthralled by their brilliant hues by day and at night by the soft, sonorous whistles with which they accompanied their amorous play. Often we stepped over them, our robes slightly cinched up, or with our feet nudged them out of the way for horrified visitors. Still we always held our guests' hands when we walked on the serpents' path; and I often noticed that the sense freedom and sure-footed confidence that filled us on this track seemed to be imparted to them as well.

Many aspects of these creatures combined to make them so familiar to us, yet we would have had but little idea of their behavior had it not been for our old cook Lampusa. Every evening, as long as summer lasted, Lampusa set out a little silver bowl of milk at the door of her kitchen carved into the cliff; then she lured the vipers with a low call. All over the garden, in the sun's last rays, we saw the golden coils gleam on the black dirt of the lily beds, on the silvery green pillows of rue, and high up in the hazel and elder bushes. Then the creatures clustered around the bowl, forming the sign of the blazing fire-wheel, and accepted the offering.

Early on, Lampusa had begun holding young Erio in her arms during this ritual and he accompanied her call in his high voice. How greatly astonished I was one evening to see the child, who had only just begun to walk, drag the bowl outside. There, he beat the rim with a pearwood spoon and the red snakes slithered, aglow, from the fissures in the Marble Cliffs. As if in a waking dream I heard little Erio laugh as he stood among them on the trodden earth of the kitchen courtyard. The creatures surrounded him, half-erect and swaying their heavy triangular heads over his in rapid pendular swings. I stood on the balcony and did not dare call out to my boy, just as when you see someone sleepwalking on a steep ridge. But then I caught sight of the old woman in the kitchen doorway—Lampusa stood smiling, her arms crossed, and I was overcome with the glorious feeling of security in the midst of mortal danger.

From that evening on it was Erio who summoned us with this vesper bell. When we heard the clink of the silver bowl, we set aside our work to rejoice in the sight of his offering. Brother Otho hurried from his library and I from the herbarium on the inner gallery. Lampusa, too, left the hearth to listen to the child, her face suffused with pride and tenderness. What amused us most was the zeal with which he kept the animals in order. Soon Erio knew each by name and he toddled among them in his little gold-trimmed, blue velvet tunic. He took great care to make sure each received its share of milk, and he made room at the bowl for the stragglers. He would tap this or that drinker on the head with his wooden spoon or, when they did not leave the bowl fast enough, he would grab them just below their heads and yank them away with all his might. However roughly he handled them, the creatures always remained gentle and tame, even when they were molting and particularly sensitive. In this season the herders do not bring their livestock to the pastures on the Marble Cliffs, for a well-aimed bite will kill even the strongest bull with lightning speed.

Erio loved the largest and most beautiful snake above all the others, the one which Brother Otho and I called the Gryphon and which, we inferred from the winegrowers' legends, had lived in the clefts since ancient times. The lance-head viper's body is a metallic red and often scales of a brassy sheen are scattered throughout the pattern on its back. But the Gryphon was marked by a flawless golden luster that turned a gemlike green near her head and shone even more intensely. When angered, she could spread her neck into a shield that glittered like a golden mirror in attack. The others seemed to show her respect, for none of them touched the bowl before the golden one had quenched her thirst. Then we watched Erio play with her while she rubbed her pointed head against his tunic, as cats are wont to do.

When it was over Lampusa served us our evening meal—two goblets of table wine and two slices of her dark, salty bread.

4.

A glass door led from the terrace to the library. In pleasant morning hours, this door stood wide open so that Brother Otho sat at his large table as if in a corner of the garden. I was always glad to enter this room where green, leafy shadows danced on the ceiling and the chirping of fledglings and the hum of bees nearby penetrated the silence.

A large drawing board was propped up on an easel near the window and along the walls shelves of books towered to the ceiling. The lowest of these was enclosed in a tall case custom-made for the larger tomes—for the oversize *Hortus Plantarum Mundi* and hand-illuminated works, the likes of which are no longer produced. This was topped by repositories that could be expanded with sliding panels—covered with stray papers and mountings of yellowed leaves from the herbarium. These dark panels also held a collection of plant fossils we had chiseled from the limestone quarries and coal pits, among them various crystals used as decorations or to weigh in one's hand during pensive conversations. Above them rose the smaller volumes—not a very extensive botanical collection but one without gaps as far as studies of lilies were concerned. This section of the library was divided into three general branches—works on form, on color, and on scent.

The bookshelves continued in the narrow hall and along the staircase that led to the herbarium. Here were kept the Church Fathers, thinkers, ancient and modern classical authors, and above all, a collection of every kind of dictionary and encyclopedia. In the evening I would meet Brother Otho in the narrow hall, where a small fire of dried vine branches flickered in the hearth. When the day's work had gone well, we would indulge in the kind of casual conversation that proceeds along well-worn paths, honoring dates and authorities along the way. We bantered over recondite trivia, over unusual quotes or those that bordered on the absurd. Our legion of mute, leather- or vellum-bound slaves served us well in these pursuits.

I usually went straight to the herbarium early and continued my work until midnight. When we moved in, we had laid a floor of thick wooden planks and set up long rows of cabinets. In their compartments thousands of herbarium sheets were stacked in bundles. We had collected only a small fraction of these; most originated from hands long ago returned to dust. Now and then, when looking for a certain plant, I would even come upon pages, browned with age, bearing a faded signature in the great Master Linnaeus's own hand. In these night and morning hours, I filled in many labels and expanded the registry—first in the collection's main catalog and then in what we called the Little Flora, in which we carefully registered all our discoveries in the region of the Marina. The following day, Brother Otho checked all the entry cards against the references, then illustrated and colored more than a few. In this way grew a work, and it was a great pleasure to us.

When we are content, even the world's most frugal gifts satisfy our senses. I have long revered the plant kingdom and traced its wonders over many years of travel. And I knew well that moment when the heart stands still at the sight of a blossoming flower, anticipating the mysteries hidden in its every seed. Nonetheless, the splendor of growth was never closer to me than in this drying room through which wafted hints of long withered greenery.

Before I lay down to rest, I would pace up and down the narrow center aisle for a short time. In these midnight hours,

I often had the impression that the plants appeared more radiant and splendid than ever before. And I caught the distant perfume of those spiny valleys adorned with white stars I had breathed in one early spring in Arabia Deserta along with the vanilla scent that refreshes the traveler in the shadeless heat of the candelabra forests. Then my memories turned again, like the pages of an old book, to hours of wild abundance—to sultry swamps in which *Victoria regia* water lilies bloomed and to littoral groves one sees smoldering in the noonday sun on bleached stilts far from the palm-fringed shore. Yet I felt none of that awe that transfixes us in the presence of nature's excessive growth, like an idol beckoning us with his thousand arms. As our study progressed, I could feel growing in me the strength to withstand and restrain the teeming powers of life—like a bridled horse.

Often dawn was already breaking before I stretched out on the narrow camp bed set up in the herbarium.

5.

Lampusa's kitchen extended into the marble cliff. Such caves had offered shepherds protection and shelter in ancient times and were later incorporated into the farmsteads like Cyclopean chambers. Very early in the morning, we would see the old woman at the fire, cooking Erio's porridge. The kitchen adjoined still deeper vaults that smelled of milk, fruit, and leaking wine. I rarely entered this part of the Rue-Herb Retreat because Lampusa's presence gave me an uneasy feeling I preferred to avoid. Erio, on the other hand, knew every inch and corner.

I often saw Brother Otho, too, standing at the old woman's side by the fire. It is to him that I owe the happiness bestowed on me by Erio, the love child of Lampusa's daughter, Silvia. At the time we were serving with the Purple Riders in a campaign against the free peoples of Alta Plana, which ultimately failed. Often, when we rode up to the passes, we would see Lampusa standing before her hut and the slender Silvia next to her in a red dress with a red kerchief on her head. Brother Otho was at my side when I picked up from the dirt the carnation Silvia had taken from her hair and thrown onto the path, and as we rode on he warned me of the old woman and the young witch—mockingly, but with an anxious undertone. Yet I was more irritated by Lampusa's laugh as she eyed me with the shameless candor of a procuress. Nonetheless, it was not long before I regularly visited her hut.

When we returned to the Marina at the end of the campaign and moved into the Rue-Herb Retreat, we learned of the child's birth and that Silvia had abandoned him and gone to live with foreigners. I found this news inopportune, coming as it did at a period in my life I had intended to devote to silent studies after the trials of the campaign.

And so I gave Brother Otho the mandate to seek out Lampusa and come to a reasonable arrangement with her. I could hardly contain my astonishment when I learned that he had immediately taken the child and her into our household; yet this step soon proved beneficial for us all. And as one recognizes a proper act in the way it also fulfills the past, so Silvia's love shone for me in a new light. I realized that I'd had a biased view of her and her mother and that I, finding her inconsequential, had treated her as such, just as one dismisses a gemstone gleaming brightly on the path as glass.

And yet everything precious comes to us by chance—the best in life costs nothing.

To be sure, straightening things out requires a broad-mindedness like Brother Otho's. His fundamental principle was to treat *everyone* we met like a rare find made on a journey. He liked to call humans *optimates*, to indicate that they are all to be counted among the natural aristocracy of this world and that every single person has excellence to offer. He held them to be vessels of wonder and accorded them, as superior beings, the rights of princes. Indeed, I saw all those we came into contact with blossom like plants waking from hibernation—it was not that they became better, but that they became more truly themselves.

Lampusa took charge of the housekeeping as soon as she moved in. She accomplished her chores with ease, and the garden flourished under her hand. While Brother Otho and I planted according to strict rules, she thrust the seeds hastily into the dirt and let the weeds grow rampant wherever they would. And still, with little effort she harvested three times the yield of our seeds and fruit. Many a time I would see her smile derisively at our beds with their oval porcelain labels indicating the genus and species painted in Brother Otho's fine hand. In doing so she bared like a tusk the last incisor she had left.

Although like Erio I called her Grandmother, Lampusa spoke to me almost exclusively of household matters, often quite foolishly, as housekeepers tend to do. Neither of us ever mentioned Silvia's name. Nonetheless I was displeased when, on the evening after the night at the town wall, Lauretta came to find me. The old woman, for her part, was especially cheerful and rushed off to fetch wine, snacks, and sweet cake for the visitor.

Through Erio I experienced the natural joys of fatherhood as well as the more spiritual pleasure of adoption. We loved his quiet, attentive character. Inclined, like all children, to imitate the work he saw around him in his small universe, Erio turned to plants at a young age. We often saw him sitting on the terrace for hours, examining a lily about to bloom, and when the bud opened, he would run into the library to delight Brother Otho with the news. Similarly, he liked to stand early in the morning at the marble basin in which we cultivated water lilies from Zipangu to hear the flower buds spring open with a delicate sound in the first rays of the sun. I also kept a chair for him in the herbarium—he often sat there and watched me as I worked. When I sensed him silently at my side, I felt invigorated, as if the deep, bright flame of life burning in his small body bathed everything in a new light. It seemed to me as well that animals sought his presence—whenever I met him in the garden, I always saw red ladybugs fluttering around him, running over his hands and playing about his hair. And it was very strange indeed that when called by Lampusa, the lancehead vipers circled the bowl in a glowing web, but with Erio they formed a disc of gleaming rays. Brother Otho noticed this first.

So it was that our lives diverged from the plans we had spun. But we saw that this divergence favored our work.

6.

We had come with the intention of studying plants in minute detail and so we began, following classical methodology, with their respiration and nutrition. Like everything on this earth, plants want to speak to us, but understanding their language requires a clear mind. Although their cycle of germination, blossoming, and wilting masks an illusion, which no created being can escape, one can still discern the eternal element locked behind the screen of appearances. Brother Otho called the art of sharpening one's vision "draining time"—yet he believed that this side of death, complete emptiness could not be achieved.

After we had settled in, we noticed that the subject of our study was expanding almost against our will. Perhaps it was the invigorating air of the Rue-Herb Retreat that steered our thinking in a new direction, just as a flame burns higher and brighter when fed pure oxygen. So, after only the first few weeks, it seemed to me that things themselves were changing, and insofar as I could not capture this transformation in words, it appeared to me at first as a lack.

When I looked out to the Marina from the terrace one morning, its water appeared deeper and more luminous, as if I were seeing it with unclouded eyes for the first time. In the very same moment, I experienced the almost painful sensation of words becoming detached from things, like strings snapping on overtaut bows. I had caught a glimpse of this world's iridescent veil, and from that very hour my tongue was no longer up to its task.

At the same time, however, I was filled with a new awareness. As children fumble for things when they first turn their eyes to the outer world, so I groped for words and images to capture this blinding new resplendence. I had never imagined that speaking could be such torment, and yet never once did I long to return to my old, naive life. Once we believe we will one day fly, an awkward leap is more precious than the security of well-trodden paths. This explains the sensation of vertigo that often came over me in my efforts.

It is easy to lose your sense of proportion when setting off into the unknown. So I was fortunate to have Brother Otho at my side as step by step we cautiously advanced. Often when I had fathomed a word, I hurried down to see him, pen in hand, and just as often he climbed up to the herbarium with the same dispatch. We also liked to create constructs, which we called "models." These were three or four sentences written in a loose meter on a sheet of notepaper. They were meant to capture a fragment of the world's mosaic, the way gems are set in metal. For these models, we used plant life as our starting point and inevitably we returned to it. In this fashion we described things and their transformation, from a grain of sand to the Marble Cliffs and from the fleeting instant to the changing seasons. In the evening we gathered these notes and, after reading them, burned them in the fireplace.

We soon felt life bring us new energy and assurance. The word is both king and conjurer. We took our measure from the elevated example of Linnaeus, who strode through the chaos of the worlds of flora and fauna with the scepter of language. And more marvelous than all empires won by the sword, his rule extended over meadows filled with wildflowers and the nameless legions of worms.

We were spurred on as well by the presentiment that order also reigns among the elements. For man is driven to imitate creation with his weak faculties just as instinct drives the bird to build its nest. Our efforts were amply rewarded with the insight that measure and law are firmly imbedded in chance and in the confusion of the natural world. In our ascent we draw ever nearer the mysteries hidden in the dust.

With every step up the mountain, the haphazard design of the horizon becomes less distinct, and when we have climbed high enough, we are surrounded by the pure ring that betroths us to eternity.

Doubtless our labors remained at the level of apprentice work and simple spelling. Nonetheless we felt growing within us the exhilaration of those who rise above the ordinary. The landscape around the Marina lost its dazzling splendor and yet shone more luminously in geometric clarity. The days flowed by with increasing rapidity and strength, like a current of water constrained by weirs. Occasionally, when the west wind blew, we had intimations of unadulterated joy.

But above all, we shook off a bit of the dread that weighed on us and, like mist rising from the swamps, clouded our minds. So it was that we did not abandon our work when the Head Forester gained power over the region and terror began to spread.

7.

We had long known of the Head Forester as an old governor of Mauretania. We'd often seen him at gatherings and spent many a night drinking and gambling with him. He was one of those figures the Mauretanians both saw as an imposing lord and considered slightly ridiculous—the way a cavalry regiment welcomes a retired colonel on occasional visits from his estates. His image was imprinted on our memory not least because of the way his green tailcoat embroidered with golden holly leaves caught every eye.

His wealth was reputed to be vast, and profusion reigned

at every banquet he hosted in his town house. His guests, as was the ancient custom, ate and drank to excess, and his great oak gaming table groaned under piles of gold. The oriental dinners he gave for his acolytes in his small villas were renowned. I had frequent opportunity, therefore, to observe him at close range, and I felt a draft of the archaic power that blew around him like a breeze from his forests. In those days, his inflexibility hardly disturbed me, for all Mauretanians acquire this mechanical bearing over time, a trait most obvious in their gaze. Accordingly, the Head Forester's eyes, too, had a glint of terrifying joviality, especially when he laughed. Like all aged drinkers' eyes, his were inflamed with a red tinge yet they also bore an expression of cunning and indomitable strength—yes, even of sovereignty at times. In those days we enjoyed his presence—we were reckless and sat at the tables of the powerful of the world.

I later heard Brother Otho say of our time with the Mauretanians that mistakes become flaws only when we persist in them. This saying struck me as all the more true when I considered the situation we were in when the Order first attracted us. There are eras of decline in which the form our inner life is destined to take becomes blurred. In these periods, we stagger this way and that like creatures who have lost their balance. We sink from hollow joys into dull sorrow, and a pervasive sense of loss lends the future and the past a more alluring air. And so we maunder through remote pasts or distant utopias while the present moment vanishes.

As soon as we became conscious of this lack, we struggled to get free. We longed for presence, for reality, and would have rushed into fire, ice, or the ether to escape the boredom. As always, when doubt combines with prodigality, we turned to force—is this not the eternal pendulum that propels the hands of time whether by day or by night? We began to dream of power and supremacy and of those forms that advance in bold ranks against each other in the deadly struggle for existence, whether bound for defeat or for victory. And we studied them avidly, the way one watches acid etch patterns on a dark mirror of polished metal. Such a penchant inevitably brought the Mauretanians to our door. We were inducted by the Capitano who had crushed the great uprising in the Iberian provinces.

Those familiar with the history of the secret orders know how difficult it is to assess their scale. They also know the way these orders rapidly proliferate in branches and colonies, such that anyone trying to track them soon gets lost in a labyrinth. This was true of the Mauretanians as well. It was especially disconcerting for the newcomer to see groups that loathed each other with deadly hatred engaged in friendly conversation in their meeting halls. One of the Mauretanians' goals was to deal artfully with world affairs. They demanded that power be wielded in a dispassionate, godlike manner, and as a result their schools dispatched a race of clear, free, and redoubtable spirits into the world. Whether they were fomenting insurrection or working with the forces of order—when they were victorious, they were victorious as Mauretanians. This Order's proud motto, SEMPER VICTRIX, did not apply to its individual members but to its guiding light, its doctrine. Amid this era's wild currents, the Order remained unwavering, and in its residences and palaces one stood on unshakable ground.

Yet it was not our preference for calm that kept us lingering there. When man loses his footing, fear takes hold and drives him blindly in its whirlwinds. Among the Mauretanians, by contrast, absolute calm reigned, as in the eye of a tornado. It is said that when you fall into the abyss, you see things with the utmost degree of clarity, as through overcorrected lenses. The air of Mauretania, fundamentally evil as it was, was the source of this sharpened vision, although without a hint of fear. When terror reigned, that is when the chill of thought and spiritual detachment increased. In the midst of catastrophes, good humor held sway and jokes abounded, like the jests of casino owners about the losses suffered by their clientele.

At the time it was clear to me that the panic whose shadow still falls over our large cities has its counterpart in the reckless arrogance of the few who circle like eagles over the mute suffering of others. Once, when we were drinking with the Capitano, he looked into his dewy goblet as into a mirror that reveals the past and mused: "No champagne will ever be more exquisite than the one they brought to us at our machines the night we burned Sagunto to the ground." And we thought: Better to perish with him than live with those who grovel in the dust out of fear.

But I digress. Among the Mauretanians you could learn those games that still amuse untrammeled spirits who have tired even of mockery. For them the world was reduced to a map like those that are engraved for amateurs using little compasses and polished instruments that are pleasing to hold. And so it seemed odd to come upon figures like the Head Forester in these clear, perfectly abstract realms free of any shadows. And yet, as soon as a free spirit establishes his hold, the native inhabitants flock to him the way snakes are drawn to an open fire. They are old connoisseurs of power who see the hour has come for them to reestablish the tyranny that has lived in their hearts from the very beginning. Thus are formed in the great orders those secret passages and tunnels no historian can penetrate. And thus are sparked the subtlest of battles aflame within the core of power: battles between images and ideas, battles between idols and the spirit.

In such conflicts, many have had to confront the source of the world's guile. That was certainly my experience when I set out in search of the missing Fortunio in the Head Forester's hunting grounds. Since that time I have known the limits that keep bold spirits in check, and so avoided stepping foot in the dark fringe of the woods the old man, whose feigned uprightness masked many snares, liked to call his "Teutoburg Forest."

8.

In my search for Fortunio, I had entered the northern edge of the forest, although our Rue-Herb Retreat lay near its southernmost point adjacent to the Burgundian land. On our return we found but a shadow of the old ways on the Marina. Until then, they had remained intact at least since Carolian times, for while foreign rulers came and went, the people who tended the grapevines there maintained their customs and their laws. And the richness, the excellence of the earth eventually mellowed even the steeliest regiment. Such is beauty's effect on power.

But the war on the borders of Alta Plana, waged like a battle against the Turks, had a deeper impact. Its ravages were like the frost that splinters the heartwood of trees with effects not visible for years. Life on the Marina followed its course. It was the old life, and yet it was somehow not the same. Occasionally, when we stood on the terrace and looked out over the encircling wreath of gardens in bloom, we caught a whiff of hidden weariness and anarchy. Those were the moments when the country's beauty touched us to the quick. Thus do life's colors flare intensely one last time before the sun sets.

In the beginning, we rarely heard of the Head Forester. Still, it was strange to see how, to the extent the weariness grew and reality became attenuated, he drew ever closer. Initially we heard only rumors, like dark reports of a pestilence raging in distant ports. Then news of nearby attacks and acts of violence spread by word of mouth until finally such deeds were committed brazenly and in the open. Just as in the mountains thick fog heralds the storm, a cloud of fear preceded the Head Forester. He was shrouded in terror, and I am convinced that this, more than the man himself, was the true source of his power. He could only act when things had already begun to falter—but once they had, with his forests he was well positioned for an attack on the land.

From the top of the Marble Cliffs, one could survey the entire expanse of the region he intended to dominate with force. To reach the pinnacle, we scaled the narrow flight of stairs carved into the rock next to Lampusa's kitchen. Worn by rain, the steps led to a protruding ledge with an unobstructed view of the surrounding land. We lingered there for many a sun-filled hour when the cliffs glowed with color because the lines etched into the dazzling white cliffs by the trickling water had taken on red and fallow hues. Thick curtains of dark ivy leaves hung down the cliff faces and the lunaria's silver leaves sparkled in the damp crevices.

On the climb our feet brushed against the red blackberry vines and frightened the jeweled lizards, which fled up to the crest in flashes of green. Where the lush grass, starred with blue gentian flowers, hung down there were clefts lined with crystals and in these hollows small owls blinked dreamily. Swift, rust-brown falcons nested there too; we passed so close to their broods, we could see the nares in their beaks, covered with a thin skin like a film of blue wax.

Up on the crest, the air was more refreshing than down on the plains where the vines trembled in the day's glare. Occasionally the heat raised a gust of wind that swept melodiously up the crag, making it resound like an organ pipe and carrying hints of roses, almond, and lemon balm. From our perch on the cliffs, we could see the roof of our hermitage far below. Toward the south, beyond the Marina, towered the mountainous region of Alta Plana, sheltered by its belt of glaciers. Its peaks were often clouded in mist that rose from the water, then the air became so clear again that we could make out the individual arolla pines that grow amid the scree at high elevations. On those days we sensed the arrival of the foehn and extinguished the fires in the house at night.

Frequently we would rest our gaze on the islands of the Marina, which we jokingly called the Hesperides, cypresses darkening their shores. Even in the harshest winter, they bear neither frost nor snow; figs and oranges ripen in the open air and roses bloom year-round. When the almond and apricot trees are in bloom, the residents of the Marina like to row across to the islands; then the islands float on the blue tides like bright flower petals. In autumn, the people embark for the islands to eat the St. Peter's fish that surface from great depths on nights of the full moon and fill the nets to bursting. The fishermen always set their nets in silence for they believe that even a whispered word will startle the schools and an oath will ruin the catch. These jaunts for St. Peter's fish were always gay affairs; one would bring along supplies of bread and wine, since the islands are not suited to wine growing. They lack the cold autumn nights when the dew forms on the grapes, enriching their mettle with a presentiment of decline.

To understand what living meant, one needed only to look to the Marina on such festive days. Early in the morning, the full range of sound drifted up to us—clearly and distinctly, the way things appear through the wrong end of a telescope. We heard the bells in the towns and gunshots fired in salute from the garlanded ships in the ports, then came the hymns of the pious throngs as they surged toward the miraculous images and the piping of flutes leading a wedding procession. We heard the calls of the jackdaws perched on the weather vanes, the crowing roosters, the cuckoo's cry, the blaring of horns blown by the hunters as they filed through the town gate on a heron hunt. These sounds drifted up, marvelous and comical, as if the world were a roguish patchwork—but also as intoxicating as wine drunk early in the day.

Far below, the Marina was wreathed with small towns whose walls and towers from Roman times were dominated by domes gray with age and Merovingian castles. Between them lay rich hamlets with flocks of pigeons circling overhead and mills covered with green moss toward which donkeys laden with sacks of wheat trotted at harvest time. Then more castles nestled on high cliff peaks along with dark-walled monasteries surrounded by carp ponds that sparkled like mirrors in the sun.

When we contemplated from our lofty seat the abodes man had built for his protection, his pleasures, his provisions and devotions, then all the eras dissolved completely into one. And the dead seemed to emerge unseen from open coffins. They are always near if we but gaze lovingly at long-cultivated lands, and just as their heritage lives on in stone and furrow, so their loyal ancestral spirits preside over field and meadow.

Behind us to the north lay the Campagna border. The Marble Cliffs separated it from the Marina like a wall. In spring, this belt of meadows spread out like a flowery carpet in which the slowly grazing herds seemed to be wading through many-colored foam. At midday, the cattle rested in the cool, marshy shade of the alders and aspens that formed leafy islands on the vast plain, from which often rose the smoke of shepherds' fires. Here and there were scattered large farmyards with stalls and barns and the tall poles of wells that filled the drinking troughs.

Summers here were very hot and hazy. In autumn, the serpents' mating season, this stretch of land was like a desert steppe, empty and sere. On its far border the Campagna turned to marshland with no sign of human habitation in the underbrush. Only a few rough reed huts built for duck hunting dotted the shore of the dark wetland lakes and a few roofed blinds were ensconced like crows' nests in the alders. The Head Forester had already established dominion here and the ground soon rose where the high forest spread its roots. From its verges, elongated shrubs, which the peasants called horns, protruded like sickles into the pastures.

This was the realm encircling the Marble Cliffs our gaze took in. From the heights we saw life itself, well cultivated and carefully trained like the vines, unfolding on ancient lands and bearing fruit. We also saw its borders: the mountain range where barbarian tribes lived in lofty freedom, though without material abundance, and toward the north the marshes and gloomy lowlands where bloody tyranny lay in wait.

Very often, when we stood side by side on the crest, we reflected on all the work that must be done before the wheat is harvested and bread is baked and on all that is necessary before the spirit can spread its wings confidently and without fear.

9.

When times were good, we paid little attention to the quarrels that had always been rife on the Campagna, and with reason, since these feuds occur wherever there are herds and pasturelands. Every spring disputes arose over cattle not yet branded, and battles broke out over watering places as soon as the dry season set in. On top of that, the massive bulls with rings in their noses, a source of terrifying dreams for the women of the Marina, forced their way into strange herds and chased them to the Marble Cliffs, at the base of which horns and ribs lay bleaching in the sun.

Above all else, the tribes of herders were ferocious and untamed. From time immemorial their trade had been passed down from father to son, and when they sat around the fire, clothed in rags and holding weapons in their fists as nature intended, the gulf that separated them from the wine-growing communities on the slopes was clear. They lived as they had in the days before houses, plows, or weaving looms were known, and sheltered in tents set up as the migration of their herds dictated. Their way of life also shaped their customs and a rude sense of justice and equality, centered solely on vengeance. Thus every killing sparked a long inferno of revenge, and some clan and family feuds exacted their tribute of blood year after year, long after the origins of the dispute were forgotten. When such suits came before Marina lawyers, they called these crude, senseless vendettas "Campagna cases"; they did not summon the herders to the forum but instead sent commissioners to their territory. In other districts it was the tenant farmers on the large estates held by magnates and overlords who were given jurisdiction. In addition, there were free herders with extensive properties, like the Bataks and the Belovars.

When dealing with the coarse tribes one also saw their admirable traits. First and foremost was the hospitality they extended to all who sat down at their fires. So it was that city faces could be seen among the herders, for the Campagna offered an initial refuge for all forced to flee the Marina. Here, in the company of renegade monks and roaming gangs, one came upon debtors facing arrest and scholars who had landed a too-sharp blow in a drinking bout. Young people thirsty for freedom and lovers longing for the shepherds' way of life were also glad to make their homes on the Campagna.

And so a web of secrecy that spanned the boundaries of the established order was constantly spun. The proximity of the Campagna, where justice was less meticulous, served these men whose affairs had taken an unfortunate turn well. Most returned after time and friends had worked to their advantage. Others disappeared into the forest never to be seen again. But after the war of Alta Plana, what had once been customary took on a sinister cast. Through sores the healthy hardly notice, the exhausted body may be seized by decay.

No one recognized the earliest signs. When rumors reached us of disturbances in the Campagna, it seemed the old blood feuds were escalating, but these were soon followed by reports of new, unfamiliar elements that were making these disputes grow darker. The core of barbarous honor that had kept violence in check disintegrated; all that remained was sheer crime. Spies and agents, it appeared, had infiltrated the allied clans in order to turn them to foreign ends. In this way, the old forms lost their meaning. When, for example, a corpse was found at a crossroad, his tongue split by a dagger, no one had ever doubted he was a traitor who had been tracked and slain in revenge. After the war, too, one came upon dead bodies similarly marked, but at that point everyone knew these were victims of pure cruelty.

Likewise, the allied clans had always exacted tributes and the landlords had paid these willingly, considering them a kind of premium for the good condition of their livestock. But the demands now swelled intolerably and when the tenant farmers saw the gleaming white of the extortion letters on the fence post, they knew they had to pay or leave the country. To be sure, many had thought of resisting, but cases of resistance were met with plundering that was clearly a strategic response.

A mob led by men from the forest would then appear outside the farm at night and, when refused entry, they rammed their way in. These bands were called "glowworms" because they broke down the doors with beams on which small lights burned. Others claimed they were given this name because after storming the gate they would torture the owners with fire to find out where the silver was hidden. In any case, we heard accounts of them committing the vilest and basest acts humans are capable of. Moreover, in order to stoke fear, they would pack their victims' dead bodies into chests or barrels and these baleful messages would be delivered with cargo from Campagna to the houses of relatives.

Still, one circumstance seemed much more ominous, and that was the fact that all these deeds that had the land up in arms and cried out for justice were rarely if ever avenged—the truth is that no one dared speak of them openly any longer since it was abundantly clear that the law was far weaker than anarchy. Commissioners accompanied by armed detachments had, in fact, been dispatched immediately after the plundering began but they found the Campagna already in complete revolt: negotiations were impossible. In order to intervene decisively, according to the constitution, they first had to convene the estates, for a country like the Marina, with a long history of law, is loath to abandon legal channels.

On this occasion it became clear that the people of the Campagna were already represented in the Marina; returning city residents had long maintained a clientele of herdsmen or had become affiliated with the clans through blood oaths. In places where order had already grown fragile these gangs soon took a turn for the worse.

Shady attorneys who defended injustice from the tribunals began to prosper, and the clansmen met openly in the small port bars. At their tables one now saw the same figures that gathered around the fires on the plains—old herdsmen, their legs wrapped in rough hides, huddled next to officers placed on half pay since Alta Plana. All those, on either side of the Marble Cliffs, who were embittered or avid for change gathered here to drink, swarming in and out as if it were their staff headquarters.

The confusion was only increased when the sons of the prominent joined in these goings-on along with young people who believed a new hour of freedom had come. Some literati began to imitate the herding songs that before had only been hummed by wet nurses from the Campagna over their charges' cradles. They strolled up and down the Corso no longer dressed in wool or linen but wearing shaggy hides, rough bludgeons in hand.

In these circles, it was the fashion to disdain the cultivation of grapes and wheat and to see the herdsmen's wild lands as the source of authentic ancestral customs. We are familiar with the confused, madcap ideas that captivate enthusiasts. It would have been easy to laugh them off had they not led to blatant sacrilege inconceivable to anyone still in possession of his reason.

10.

In the Campagna, one often saw the herders' small gods standing where the grazing trails crossed district lines. These guardians of limits were roughly hewn from stone or old oak wood, and even from a distance they gave off a rancid odor. Traditional offerings consisted of libations of melted butter and intestinal fat scraped off with the sacrificial knife. This was why black scars of small fires dotted the green pastures around the idols. Their offerings completed, the herdsmen kept a charred stick, which they would use on the night of the solstice to mark all the bodies of those meant to bear young, their women and cattle alike.

When we encountered young maids returning from milking at such spots, they would cover their faces with their headscarves, and Brother Otho, friend and connoisseur of garden gods, never passed the idols without paying them mocking homage. He claimed they were very ancient deities and called them Jupiter's childhood companions.

There was also, not far from the Flayer's Horn, a copse of weeping willows in the midst of which there stood the effigy of a steer with red nostrils, a red tongue, and his member painted bright red. It was a place of ill repute and rumors of appalling celebrations were associated with it.

Yet who would have believed that the gods of fat and butter who filled the cows' udders would gain a following in the Marina—of worshippers, at that, who came from houses in which offerings and sacrifices had long been mocked? The same spirits who deemed themselves strong enough to cut the ties that bound them to their ancestral faith became subjugated to the barbarian idols' spell. The sight of their blind obedience was more repugnant than drunkenness at midday. They believed and boasted that they could fly but they merely scrabbled in the dirt.

Also disquieting was the way this confusion encroached on the rites honoring the dead. In the Marina, poets had been held in great esteem throughout the ages. They were considered generous benefactors and the gift of writing verse was regarded as the source of their wealth. That the grapevines bloomed and bore fruit, that men and cattle prospered, that evil winds dispersed and joyous concord filled all hearts— all of this was ascribed to the harmonious words that came to life in song and hymns. Even the most modest vintner was convinced of this, as he was of the healing powers of harmony.

None was so poor that he did not bring the first and best fruits of his garden to the thinkers' huts and poets' cells. Thus anyone who felt a calling to serve the world through his intellect could live a life of leisure—in poverty, to be sure, but without want. For the exchanges between those who tilled fields and those who cultivated words this old adage was held as a precept: The gods' best gifts are given for free.

One sign of great eras is that the power of the spirit is visible and manifest in them. That was the case here: In the change of seasons, in religious observances, and in human life, no festival was possible without poetry. Most important, however, was the poet's role in funeral rites: after the corpse was blessed, the poet's office was to judge the dead. It was incumbent on him to cast a godlike eye over the vanished life and exalt it in verse, like a diver extracting the pearl from its shell.

From earliest times there had been two degrees of honor accorded to the dead, the elegeion being more common one. The elegeion was considered a fit offering for an honest life lived in sorrow and in joy, our human fate. Its tone was one of lament but with an assurance that offered solace to the grieving heart.

Then there was the eburnum, reserved in antiquity for slayers of monsters that dwelt in swamps and ravines before there were human settlements. The classical eburnum was delivered in a tone of refined, elevated joy; it concluded with an admiratio, during which a black eagle rose from a broken cage and soared into the air. As times became less harsh, eburnums were granted to those called builders or "optimates." The people always had a sure instinct for who belonged among these ranks, although as life became more refined, their ancestral images changed with them.

But now, for the first time, disputes arose over the speeches delivered by the judges of the dead. The clans had brought their blood feuds from the Campagna to the towns. Hatred swelled like a plague on unprotected ground. People attacked each other at night with the vilest of weapons for no other reason than that Jegor had murdered Wenzel a hundred years before. But what need is there for reasons when blindness overcomes us? Before long, not a single night passed without the watch finding dead bodies, on the streets and in houses, many bearing wounds unworthy of the sword—indeed, sometimes even wounds inflicted by blind rage on an enemy already dead.

In these clashes, which led to manhunts, ambushes, and arson, the parties lost all restraint. Soon it seemed that they barely saw each other as human, and their speech became laden with words reserved for such vermin as were to be wiped out, exterminated, and fumigated. They only recognized murder when committed by the opposing side and they praised acts committed by their own that they decried from their foes. Whereas all deemed the others' dead barely worth burying in the dark of night, their own merited the purple shroud, the eburnum song, and the eagle soaring to the gods, living symbol of heroes and prophets.

Of course, none of the great singers was willing to be a part of such profanation despite being proffered piles of gold. So each side turned to the harpists who played for dances at the yearly fairs and the blind zither players who delighted the drunken guests outside the triclinia in houses of pleasure with songs about Venus's scallop shell or gluttonous Hercules. Now the battlers and bards were equals.

But meter, as is known, cannot be bribed. The fires of destruction cannot touch its invisible pillars and gates. Those swindlers who believed that offerings of the eburnums' rank could be bought were themselves duped. We attended only the first few of these obsequies and saw exactly what we had expected. The hireling who was meant to follow the poem's sublime, illuminated arc immediately began to stammer and lost his way. His words regained their fluency and debased themselves to vindictive, vengeful iambs that writhed in the dust. At these spectacles we saw the crowd clad in the red robes worn for eburnums. The magistrates and clergy in their regalia were there too. In other times, silence reigned when the eagle rose but now wild cheering broke out.

We were filled with grief at these sounds, as were many others. We felt that the benevolent ancestral spirits had abandoned the Marina.

II.

There were many other signs of manifest decline. They resembled a rash that appears, clears up, and erupts again. There were also stretches of cheerful days when everything seemed to be as before.

Precisely this was one of the Head Forester's masterly traits: he spread fear in small doses, which he then gradually increased, with the aim of paralyzing resistance. The role he played in this turmoil, planned in minute detail in his forests, was that of a force of order, for while his lower agents, members of the herders' clans, extended the reach of anarchy, his adepts infiltrated the ministries and courts, even the monasteries, and were seen there as powerful figures who would bring the rabble to heel. In this the Head Forester was like an evil doctor who inflicts an ailment in order to subject the patient to his intended surgery.

While there were a few magistrates clear-sighted enough

to see through his game, they lacked the power to stop him. In the Marina the state had long relied on troops of foreign mercenaries and as long as order reigned it was well served. But now that conflicts encroached upon its shores, the mercenaries were in great demand and the prestige of their leader, Biedenhorn, increased enormously overnight. He was surely the last to want to interfere with a change so favorable to his interest; instead he made difficulties, keeping his troops for himself, like capital earning interest. He holed up with them in an old fortress, the Bulwark, where he lived high on the hog. He built a banquet hall in the vault of the great tower and drank comfortably ensconced inside the walls. The window's stained glass sported his crest, two drinking horns with the motto PASS YE ROUND THE WELCOME QUAFF.

He lived in this refuge, filled with the jovial cunning of Northerners, which is often underestimated, hearing out complaints with well-feigned concern. Glass in hand, he carried on zealously about justice and order—but no one saw him strike a blow for either. At the same time, he negotiated not only with the clans but also with the Head Forester's captains, whom he wined and dined at the Marina's expense. With these forest captains he played a dirty trick on the local authorities. Claiming he was in need of assistance, he handed control over the rural districts to them and their forest ruffians. So terror established its reign behind a mask of order.

The contingents allotted to the captains were small at first, dispatched one by one as mounted troops. We often saw these huntsmen passing by the Rue-Herb Retreat, and unfortunately they would stop for a bite in Lampusa's kitchen. These were unmistakably forest rabble, short and squinting, with dark tangled beards hanging from their gaunt faces;

they spoke a thieves' jargon that had taken the worst of every tongue and seemed to be molded out of blood-crusted dirt.

We found them armed with paltry weapons, with slings, nets, and the curving daggers they called blood-tappers; they were also usually hung with the pelts of smaller animals. They stalked the large jeweled lizards on our steps up the Marble Cliffs; they caught them the old-fashioned way, by moistening a fine snare with spit. We had often delighted at the sight of these beautiful, gleaming, golden-green creatures, especially when we spotted them in the blackberry bushes that spread a web of red tendrils over the cliffs. The skins were coveted by the southern courtesans the old man tolerated on his farms and were thus in great demand; his muscadins and spintrians had them made into belts and sheaths. As a result, these enchanting green creatures were relentlessly hunted and were the victims of appalling horrors. Indeed, these torturers did not even bother to kill them but skinned them alive, then let them fall from the cliffs like white shadows, to die in terrible agony at the foot of the cliffs. The hatred of beauty burns deep within the basest hearts.

Such carrion-hunting side jobs were simply a pretext to spy on farms and houses and see if a spark of freedom still burned in any of them. Then the acts of banditry, already familiar from the Campagna, resumed and the inhabitants were taken away under cover of darkness and fog. Not one of them returned and the rumors that spread about their fate reminded us of the ill-used jeweled lizard cadavers we found at the foot of the cliffs and filled our hearts with grief.

Then came the foresters, who were often to be seen at work in the vineyards and on the slopes. They seemed to be surveying the land anew, since they had holes dug in the ground and erected poles covered with runes and animal totems. The way they moved over the fields and meadows was even more dismaying than the movements of the hunters, for the foresters prowled land that had been cultivated for generations as if it were heath, respecting neither paths nor boundaries. Nor did they honor the sacred images with a greeting. We saw them cross the rich fields as if they were barren, unconsecrated wastelands.

From such signs we could surmise what to expect from the old man, lurking deep within his forests. With his hatred of the plow, grain, grape, and domesticated animals and his revulsion for spacious estates and life lived openly in the light of day, he had no interest in reigning over such abundance. His heart warmed only when moss and ivy turned ruined cities green and when bats fluttered in the moonlight around the cathedral's broken cross vaults. He wanted to see the trees of his domain extend to the Marina's shore and bathe their roots in its water and to see above their crowns the silver egret meet the black stork flying from the oak stands to the marshland. He wanted tusked wild boars to root in the rich black earth of the vineyards and beavers to swim in the monastery ponds when large herds of game followed hidden paths to quench their thirst at dusk. And along the edges, where trees could not take root in the marshes, he wanted to see the snipe take flight in spring and the thrush peck at the red berries in late autumn.

12.

The Head Forester had no affection for farmsteads or poets' haunts either, nor for any place of calm reflection. The best his territory had to offer was a breed of rude knaves who lived only for tracking and hunting, all of them, father to son, entirely devoted to the old man. These were his master huntsmen, whereas the subordinate hunters we saw at the Marina came from strange villages the old man supported deep within his forest.

Fortunio, who knew the old man's dominion best, described these villages to me as jumbles of dilapidated gray hovels with walls built of clay and chaff and pointed roofs covered with sallow moss. A dark brood of outlaws lived in these cave-like homes. When these nomad clans were on the move, they always left behind a vestige of themselves in their nests and dens, the way a final remnant is always kept in a pepper pot to flavor the next batch.

In these forest depths, all those who fled extermination in times of war or times of peace found shelter—Huns, Tatars, Gypsies, Albigensians, and heretical sects of every sort. They were joined by fugitives from the military police or the executioner's hand, scattered clusters of the great robber bands of Poland and the Lower Rhine, and women who no longer work with their hands, those wenches bailiffs chase from before the gates.

Necromancers and warlocks who had escaped the stake also established their dens of magic here; and for the initiated, for Venetians and alchemists, these unknown villages counted as havens of the black arts. Once, in Fortunio's hands, I saw a manuscript by Rabbi Nilufer, who—having been expelled from Smyrna—had also been a guest in these forests on his wanderings. In his writings one saw that world history was reflected here as in murky ponds, on the banks of which rats build their nests. The manuscript also held the key to many dark mysteries; it reported, for example, that after he was banished from Perouard, Master Villon had found refuge deep in this forest, where the Coquillards along with many another band of brigands had their headquarters. They later established themselves in Burgundy, but always kept a bolt-hole here.

Whatever dross the world poured into its depths, the forest returned with compound interest from its womb. It was the main seedbed of those servile huntsmen who volunteered to exterminate the vermin from house and field— it was here and nowhere else, according to Nilufer, that the Piper from Hamlin had disappeared with the children. With these bands pillage and strife swept back and forth across the land. But from these forests also came those graceful swindlers who appear with coaches and servants, whom one meets even in princely courts. A dark stream of blood flowed from the forest into the channels of the world. Wherever crimes and depravities were committed, one of these sinister bands was always present—and they joined the dance when the wind on the gibbet hills led the poor villains in a farandole.

For every one of them, the old man was the great master; they kissed the hem of his red hunting jacket or his bootleg when he sat astride his horse. He treated them capriciously in turn, stringing a few dozen up in the trees like fieldfare when they seemed to spawn too profusely. Otherwise he let them nest and feast on his lands as they would.

As patron of this vagrants' homeland, the Head Forester wielded a vast, widely branching, hidden web of power in the outside world. Wherever structures of human order were fragile, his brood spread like fungus over the land. They swarmed and stirred things up where servants refused allegiance to the ancestral lines, where mutiny broke out on

storm-tossed ships, where soldiers deserted king and commander in battle.

No one but the Head Forester was well served by these
forces. When he welcomed Mauretanians in his town house,
he was attended by a crowd of servants—by hunters in green
livery, by footmen in red tailcoats and black court shoes, and
by all manner of clerks and confidants. At these feasts there
was some sense of the comfort the old man liked to surround
himself with in his forests. The large room was warm and
well lit—not by sunlight, but rather by the flickering light
of flames and the gold that gleams in caves.

Like resplendent diamonds amid base glowing embers in
the alchemist's crucible, women of exquisite beauty occasionally grew up in these forest dens. These women were, like all
the forest dwellers, in bondage to the Head Forester, and on
his travels he always brought several palanquins along in his
cortege. When he invited young Mauretanians to his small
houses outside the town gates and was in good humor, he
might display his odalisques as others do their treasures. He
had them summoned to his billiards room, where he and his
guests gathered after a heavy meal to drink a ginger brew, and
he gave the women balls to play a round. The men then watched
the exposed bodies as they leaned over the green tables in the
red glow of the lamps, slowly bending and twisting themselves
into various poses the game requires. From his forests came
reports of much cruder things in this regard, of how, after a
long hunt for fox, elk, or bear, he held drinking parties on
the threshing floor adorned with guns and antlers and sat
enthroned on a dais surrounded by blood-soaked game.

These women also served as the most refined of lures
wherever he pursued his worldly intrigues. Whoever approached these treacherous blossoms that had sprouted in

the swamp fell under the enchantment that incurs abasement. In our time in Mauretania, we saw many men of great promise and destiny succumb—for noble spirits are the first to be snared by these wiles.

Such was the human stock that was going to populate the region when it fell completely under the old man's dominion, just as the crab apple, the poppy, and henbane succeed noble fruits when the enemy lays waste to the gardens. Then the generous deities of wine and bread would be replaced on the pedestals by strange gods—like Diana, degenerated to rampant fertility in the swamps, flaunting grapelike clusters of golden breasts, and along with her, dreadful icons that terrify with their claws, horns, and teeth and demand sacrifices unworthy of men.

13.

This is how things stood seven years after the battle of Alta Plana, and we attributed to that military campaign all the evil that had darkened the land. To be sure, we had both taken part and had joined in the carnage with the Purple Riders at the entrance to the mountain passes—but only to fulfill our feudal duty, and as such it was incumbent on us to strike, not to ponder right and wrong. Yet, just as the arm is more readily commanded than the heart, our spirit sided with the people so bravely defending their hereditary freedom against domination, and we saw their victory as more than the fortunes of war.

We had also won a hospitable friend in Alta Plana because Ansgar, the son of the Bodan Alps tavern keeper, had fallen into our hands before the passes and exchanged gifts with us. From our terrace we could see the Bodan Alps tavern far in the distance, like a patch of blue nestled deep in the sea of snowy peaks, and the thought that at any hour in that high valley there was a place, a refuge prepared for us as for a brother, filled us with a sense of security.

When we returned to our native land far in the north and stored our weapons in the armory, we longed for a life washed clean of violence, and we recalled our former studies. We reported to the Mauretanians to request an honorable leave from their ranks and we received the black-red-black ribbon of retired veterans. We surely lacked neither the courage nor the power of judgment needed to reach a high rank in this Order. But we never had the talent for looking down on the suffering of the nameless and the weak the way senators look down at the arena from their seats on the tribune. But what is to be done when the weak ignore the law and, in their blindness, undo the locks and bolts that had been secured for their protection? We could not, therefore, place all the blame on the Mauretanians, for right and wrong were now fully intermingled; the stoutest hearts wavered, and the time was ripe for the forces of terror. In this the human order resembles the cosmos—from time to time it must be engulfed in flame in order to be born anew.

We were surely right to avoid affairs from which no honor could be won and to return to the peace of the Marina and, on its luminous shores, to devote our attention to flowers, those ephemeral, many-colored symbols which contain the immutable, like a secret hieroglyphics, and which resemble clocks that always tell the right time.

Yet our house and garden had scarcely been set up and our work only advanced enough to show its first fruits when the glow of arson smoldered on the Campagna side of the Marble Cliffs. When the unrest spread to the Marina, we had to gather intelligence to keep ourselves informed of the extent and nature of the threat.

Old Belovar, whom we jokingly called the Arnaut, lived on the Campagna and was often to be found in Lampusa's kitchen. He brought herbs and rare roots that his wives dug up from the rich earth of the prairies and Lampusa dried them for her brews and concoctions. For this reason we had befriended him and emptied many jugs of wine with him on the kitchen courtyard bench. Belovar's knowledge of the folk names for a vast array of flowers was impeccable; and we gladly listened to him to enrich our synonymy. He also knew where rare species grew—like the lizard orchid, with flowers that smell of goat, that blooms among the bushes; the man orchid, with labella shaped like the human body; and the bee orchid, with a flower like a panther's eye. So it was that we often invited him to accompany us when we collected specimens on the far side of the Marble Cliffs. He knew all the paths and trails up to the forest's edge; but most importantly, when the herdsmen became unruly, his presence proved to be reliable protection.

This old man embodied the best the pastureland had to offer—admittedly not in the fashion dreamed of by the muscadins. These fops believed they had discovered the ideal man among the herding tribes, whom they praised in rose-tinted poems. Old Belovar was seventy, his body was tall and lean, and his white beard contrasted strangely with his black hair. His most striking feature was his dark eyes, which were as sharp and piercing as a falcon's, though in anger they flashed like a wolf's. He wore gold hoops in his ears. He also wore a red scarf and a belt of red cloth from which emerged the pommel and point of a dagger. Eleven notches, stained red with madder, were carved into the handle of this old weapon.

When we first met him, the old man had just taken his third wife, a young woman of sixteen, whom he kept under strict control and no doubt beat when he was drunk. When he got onto the topic of vendetta feuds, his eyes began to flash and we understood that an enemy's heart drew him like an irresistible magnet for as long as it beat; and the afterglow of revenge made him a bard, of which there were so many on the Campagna. When they drank to the honor of herder gods around the fire there, it often happened that one of the men in the circle would rise and, in inspired words, vaunt of the mortal blow he had dealt his enemy.

Over time we became attached to the old man and were glad to see him, the way you put up with a faithful dog even though a wolfish nature still burns within it. A fierce, elementary fire blazed within this man, yet there was nothing ignominious about him, and that is why he despised the dark forces issuing from the forest and spreading over the Campagna. We soon noticed that this unrefined soul was not without virtue; the good burned more ardently in him than in any of the towns. As a result, friendship was more than sentiment to him; it flared up as instinctively and indomitably as hatred. We realized this when in the courts, not long after we had arrived, Brother Otho managed to turn a disagreeable affair in which the consuls of the Marina had embroiled Belovar to the old man's advantage. From that point on we had a firm place in his heart and his eyes lit up even when he saw us from afar.

We soon learned to take care not to express any wish in his presence, for he would have braved the Gryphon's nest to delight us with its young. We could call on him at any time, like a trusty weapon always at hand; and through him we tasted the power of having someone completely devoted to us, a power that is waning as civilization develops.

This friendship alone made us feel well protected against the dangers threatening us from the Campagna. Many nights we sat working silently in the library and herbarium, while the flames of arson blazed on the edge of the cliffs. Often the strife came so near that the north wind carried the sounds of destruction up to our retreat. We heard the blows of battering rams on farm gates and the bellowing of the livestock caught in flaming stalls. The wind also carried the soft hum of voices and the pealing of bells in the private chapels—and when it all suddenly fell silent, we still harkened for it late into the night.

But we knew that no harm threatened our Rue-Herb Retreat as long as the old herdsman and his fierce tribe were down on the steppe.

14.

On the Marina side of the Marble Cliffs, on the other hand, we could count on the support of Father Lampros, a Christian monk from the Maria Lunaris monastery, which was revered among the people as the Falcifera. These two men, the herdsman and the monk, clearly showed the diversity of influence that different native soils exert as much on men as on plants. The old blood avenger was inhabited by pasturelands still unfurrowed by the plowshare's iron, as in the priest there lived the glebe of vineyards, rendered as fine as the sand in an hourglass by the care of human hands over many centuries.

Word of Father Lampros first came to us from Upsala, specifically through Ehrhardt, who worked there as custodian of the herbarium and supplied us with material for our studies. At the time, we were occupied with the way plants arrange their parts like radii in a circle, organized around an axis, which is the basis of all organic forms, and ultimately with the process of crystallization and the way in which it invariably gives meaning to growth, as the clock's face gives meaning to the hands. Ehrhardt informed us that nor far from us on the Marina lived the author of a fine work on the symmetry of fruits—a certain Phyllobius, a pen name that masked Father Lampros's identity. This news sparked our curiosity, and, after sending him a note, we visited the monk in the monastery of the Falcifera.

This monastery was so close that we could see the point of its tower from the Rue-Herb Retreat. The church was a pilgrimage site and the path to it led through gentle meadows on which the old trees bloomed so magnificently that barely a single green leaf showed amid the white. In the morning, not a soul was to be seen in the gardens cooled by breezes from the lake and yet the vitality of the blossoms and the charged air had such an effect on our spirits that we felt as if we were walking through enchanted gardens. Soon we saw on the hill before us the monastery, with its church built in a cheerful style. Even from a distance we could hear the organ accompanying the pilgrims' hymns in veneration of the icon.

When the porter led us through the church, we too paid our respects to the miraculous image. We saw the woman exalted and seated on a throne of clouds, her feet resting, as on a stool, upon a thin crescent moon with a face gazing at the earth fashioned in the inner curve. This deity, revered as the source and dispenser of all things, was thus depicted as the power that rules impermanence.

In the cloister, we were welcomed by the circator, a prior who led us to the library supervised by Father Lampros. This is where he spent the hours designated for work and where, surrounded by large tomes, we often lingered and talked with him. The first time we stepped through the doors we saw the Father, who had just come in from the monastery garden, standing in the silent room, a carmine gladiolus stem in his hand. He was still wearing his large beaver hat, and the colorful light that fell through the tracery window danced over his white robe.

In Father Lampros we found a man around fifty years old, of medium height and slender build. As we approached him, we were filled with trepidation, since his face and hands were singular and disconcerting. It seemed, if I may put it this way, as if they belonged to a corpse, and it was difficult to imagine there was any life or blood in them. They appeared to have been shaped from soft wax—and his facial expressions surfaced very slowly, more as a shimmer than a movement of his features. He also appeared strangely rigid and symbolic when he raised his hand in conversation, as he was wont to do. And yet his body moved with an easy grace that seemed to enter him like breath bringing a puppet to life. And he did not lack for merriment.

When greeting him, Brother Otho praised the sacred image by noting that he saw in it the grace of Fortuna and that of Vesta united in a superior form—at which the monk lowered his head politely and then raised it to face us with a smile. It was as if he had received these few words, after reflecting upon them, as a pilgrim's offering.

From this and many other traits we recognized that Father Lampros avoided argument; his silences were more powerful than his words. In science as well, in which he was deemed among the masters, he did not take part in the disputes between the various schools. His principle was that each theory was a contribution to genesis because in every era human intelligence conceives creation anew—and that each interpretation contains no more truth than a leaf that unfolds and soon withers. That is the reason he called himself Phyllobius, "he who lives among leaves," in his unusual characteristic mixture of modesty and pride.

Father Lampros's dislike of contradiction was also a sign of the courtesy so highly refined in his nature. Being intellectually superior as well, he would receive his interlocutor's words and return them in a way that confirmed in them a higher meaning. Accordingly, his response to Brother Otho's greeting revealed not only the goodness the cleric had acquired over the years and enhanced like a fine wine but also the courtesy cultivated in noble houses and imbued in their offspring as a second, milder nature. There was pride in his nature too—for those who rule have a firm sense of judgment and place no stock in opinions.

It was rumored that Father Lampros came from an old Burgundian family, but he never spoke of the past. From his time in the world he had retained only a signet ring; its carnelian stone was engraved with a gryphon's wing and the motto PATIENCE IS MINE. This too displayed the two poles of his nature—modesty and pride.

We soon began frequent visits to the monastery of the Falcifera, lingering in the flower garden or in the library. Before long our florula was greatly enriched, for Father Lampros had been collecting plants on the Marina for many years and we never left without a bundle of herbarium sheets captioned in his own hand, each a small work of art.

These conversations also proved fruitful to our work on axial growth, since it is crucial to the development of any project to weigh it with a discerning mind from time to time. In this respect we had the impression that the monk was collaborating with us on our work without any desire for authorial recognition. Not only did he possess enormous knowledge of phenomena, but he also knew how to elicit those rare moments when the meaning of our own work was revealed to us in a flash.

One morning, for example, Father Lampros led us over a flower-covered slope, which the monastery gardeners had been hoeing earlier that day, to a spot covered by a red cloth. He told us that he had spared from the hoe a plant that would delight us, but when he removed the cloth we saw nothing more than a young shrub in the plantain family of the sort Linnaeus had named *Plantago major*, a plant found on every path human foot has ever trod. However, when we bent down and examined it more closely, it appeared to have grown unusually large and evenly; oval leaves divided its circumference into a serrated green circle from the center of which rose its gleaming point of growth. The freshness and delicacy of the plant's living tissue was matched by the incorruptible genius of its symmetry. A shudder ran through us; we felt how closely the desire for life and the desire for death were united within us; and when we stood up again, we looked into Father Lampros's smiling face. He had entrusted us with a mystery.

We treasured the moments of leisure Father Lampros offered us, because his name was revered among the Christians and many sought him out for counsel and consolation. And yet he was also loved by those who worshipped the twelve gods and by those who came from northern lands where the Aesir are honored in vast halls and enclosed sacred groves. Father Lampros ministered to them from this same strength when they came to him, but not as a priest. Brother Otho, who knew many temples and mysteries, often said that the most wonderful aspect of his spirit was his ability to ally such a high level of knowledge with the observation of strict rules. Brother Otho believed that dogma accompanies spirituality along its progressive refinement—like a robe that is interwoven with gold and purple thread in the early stages and gains an invisible quality with each step until the pattern gradually dissolves into light.

Because Father Lampros was trusted by all the powers operating in the Marina, he was privy to the course of all events. He no doubt had a more comprehensive view of the game being played there than anyone else, and so it seemed strange to us that he did not allow any of it to encroach on his monastic life. In fact, it seemed that the closer danger approached, the clearer and brighter his inner light shone.

We often spoke of him as we sat by a fire of vine clippings in our hermitage, for in times of great threat such men tower over the wavering generations. Now and again we wondered if he felt the corruption had advanced too far to be remedied or if modesty and pride prevented him from interfering in the parties' battles through word or deed. Yet Brother Otho described the situation best when he said that destruction holds no terror for natures like his, which are made to enter the highest flames as if stepping into one's own familial house. Father Lampros, living like a dreamer behind the monastery walls, was perhaps the only one of us to live at the heart of reality.

Be that as it may—while Father Lampros disdained safety

for his own account, he was faithful in his concern for us. He often sent us notes signed Phyllobius urging us to set off on an excursion to this or that place where some rare flower was in bloom. We suspected then that he wanted to be sure we were in some distant spot at a certain hour and so we acted accordingly. He no doubt chose this form of communication because he learned many things in inviolable confidence.

We also noticed that when we were not in the Rue-Herb Retreat, he sent these messages through Erio, not through Lampusa.

15.

When the fires of destruction raged at the foot of the Marble Cliffs, memories of our time with the Mauretanians awoke in us and we weighed the possibility of resorting to violence. The several powers in the Marina still held each other in such a delicate equilibrium that weaker powers could upset the balance, for as long as the clans fought each other and Biedenhorn and his mercenaries behaved equivocally, the Head Forester had few men at his disposal.

We considered joining Belovar and his clan in their nighttime raids on the hunters and hanging by the crossroads the lacerated corpses of those we snared, for this was to speak with the brutes from the forest villages in the only language they understood. When we discussed such plans with him, out of sheer delight the old man bounced his broad dagger up and down in its sheath as if in amorous play and urged us to sharpen the jaws of our foothold traps and starve our hounds until the scent of blood had their red tongues hanging to the ground. Then we too felt the force of instinct course through our bodies like a flash of lightning.

But when we discussed the situation more thoroughly in the herbarium or in the library, we strengthened our resolve to resist solely through the power of the spirit. After Alta Plana, we believed we had discovered weapons stronger than those that slash or stab, yet, like children, we occasionally fell back on that primitive world in which terror is all-powerful. We did not yet know the full extent of man's power.

In this regard, our interaction with Father Lampros was invaluable to us. Had we listened only to our own hearts, we would no doubt have resolved to act in the same spirit in which we returned to the Marina; but at such turns in life, help comes from another. The presence of a good teacher makes our most fundamental wishes clear to us and enables us to be ourselves. That is why these noble images are deeply imprinted in our hearts; through them we intuit what we are capable of.

A strange period on the Marina began for us then. While evil spread across the land like fungus on a rotten log, we delved ever deeper into the mystery of flowers, and their calyxes seemed larger and more vibrant than usual. But above all we pursued our work on language, because in the word we recognized the gleam of the magical blade before which the tyrant's power pales. Word, spirit, and freedom form a trinity.

I daresay that our efforts bore fruit. Many mornings we woke with great cheer and savored the taste of well-being granted those in the best of health. On those days we had no difficulty finding names for things and we moved through the Rue-Herb Retreat as if the rooms were filled with magnetic energy. We strode through the chambers and the garden in a subtle, heady intoxication and sometimes placed our notes on the mantelpiece.

On such days, we would climb to the top of the cliffs when the sun was high. We stepped over the dark hieroglyphs of the lancehead vipers on the serpents' path and ascended the stairs that shimmered brightly in the sun. From the highest ridge of the cliffs, which spread their blinding whiteness far in the midday sun, we contemplated the land for a long time, searching for its salvation in every fold and every line. Then, as if scales had fallen from our eyes, we perceived its imperishable splendor, like that of things preserved in poetry.

The knowledge that destruction does not abide in the elements, but instead that its illusion merely hovers over their surface like veils of mist that cannot withstand the sun filled us with joy. And we felt that if we could live in those indomitable cells, then we would pass through each phase of annihilation as if exiting the open doors of one banquet hall into ever more splendid ones.

When we stood thus on the crest of the Marble Cliffs, Brother Otho would often say that this was the meaning of life: reenacting creation in the ephemeral, the way a child at play imitates his father's work. What gives meaning to sowing and procreation, to building and establishing order, to images and poetry, is that the masterwork is reflected in them as in a mirror of multicolored glass that soon shatters.

16.

We look back with pleasure on our proudest days. But we must not pass silently over those times in which baser powers had the upper hand. In hours of weakness, destruction takes on a terrible aspect, like the images one sees in the temples of vengeful deities.

Many a morning dawned while we paced apprehensively through the Rue-Herb Retreat or daydreamed morosely in the herbarium and the library. On those days we would close the shutters tight and read by lamplight yellowed pages and manuscripts that had accompanied us on our many voyages. We also pored over old letters and for consolation paged through treasured books in which hearts long since turned to dust still warmed our own. In the same way, the heat of earthly summers is preserved in dark veins of coal.

On these days darkened by ill humor, we closed the doors that opened onto the garden because we found the flowers' fresh scent too caustic. In the evening we would send Erio to the cliff kitchen to have Lampusa fill a pitcher with wine pressed in the year of the comet.

Then, with the vine branches burning in the fireplace, we followed a custom we had adopted in Britain and set out amphorae of perfume. For these we gathered flower petals in their seasons and after drying them, pressed them in wide-bellied vessels. When we lifted the lids from the pots in wintertime, the colorful flowers had long since faded into shades of yellowed silk and pale purple fabric. A faint, lovely fragrance rose from this flowery aftermath like the memory of mignonette beds and rose gardens.

On these melancholy celebrations we also lit heavy candles made of beeswax. They came from the parting gift bestowed on us by the Provençal knight Deodat, killed many years earlier in wild Taurus. In their light, we reminisced about this noble friend and the evening hours we had whiled away in conversation with him on the high walls of Rhodes as the sun set in the cloudless Aegean sky. As it sank, a mild breeze blew into the city from the empty galley port. The roses' sweet scent mingled with the odor of the fig trees, and the essence of distant wooded and herb-covered slopes fused in the sea breeze. But most intense of all, a lush, exquisite smell rose from the rampart trenches, where yellow tufts of chamomile bloomed.

With the smell, the last bees, heavy with pollen, ascended and flew through the slits in the walls and the crenellations on the battlements, returning to their hives in the small gardens. Their drunken buzzing had so often enthralled us as we stood on the bastion of the Gate d'Amboise that Deodat gave us a load of their wax to take with us when we parted ways—"so that you never forget the golden humming on the island of roses." And truly, when the candles were lit, there radiated from the wicks a delicate, dry aroma of spices and the perfume of the flowers that bloom in the Saracen gardens.

So we raised a glass to old and distant friends and to the countries of this world. Trepidation comes over us all when the winds of death blow. Then we eat and drink, wondering how much longer we will have a place at the table. For ours is a beautiful world.

Another thought weighed on us as well, one familiar to all those engaged in the work of the mind. We had devoted many a year to our plant studies, sparing no effort or lamp oil. We had also gladly sacrificed our inheritance to it. Now the first ripe fruits were falling into our laps. For here were the letters, manuscripts, commonplace books, and herbaria, the war and travel diaries, and especially our materials on language—many thousands of fragments assembled like small stones in a mosaic now far advanced. We had only published a small fraction of these manuscripts, because

Brother Otho maintained that playing music for the deaf was bad craftmanship. We lived in an age that condemned authors to solitude. And yet, we would gladly have seen much of our work published—not for posthumous fame, no less a form of illusion than the fleeting instant, but because print bears the seal of completion and permanence, the sight of which gladdens even the most solitary heart. We take leave more easily when our things are in order.

When we worried over the fate of our papers, we often thought of Phyllobius's smiling serenity. We lived very differently in the world. Being separated from the works in which we had woven a part of ourselves and set down roots seemed to us far too difficult to bear. Still, for consolation we had the mirror of Nigromontanus, the sight of which always raised our spirits in despondent moods. It was part of my old teacher's bequest and it had the property of concentrating the sunlight that passed through it into a fire of extreme intensity. Things set alight by such heat became imperishable in a way Nigromontanus said could best be compared to pure distillation. He had learned this art in the monasteries of the Far East where the treasures of the dead are burned so they will accompany their owners through all eternity. He similarly maintained that everything set aflame by this mirror was preserved more securely in the realm of the invisible than behind any armored door. It would be transposed through a flame that showed neither smoke nor base reddening to a realm beyond destruction. Nigromontanus called it security in the void, and we resolved to summon it when the hour of annihilation was upon us.

We treasured the mirror like a key to a higher chamber and on those evenings we would carefully open the blue case that held it in order to rejoice in its sparkling. Framed with a ring of electrum, its disc of clear rock crystal shone in the candlelight. Into this rim Nigromontanus had engraved, using sun runes, a motto worthy of his boldness.

AND SHOULD THE EARTH BURST LIKE A SHOT,
OUR TRANSFORMATION WILL BE IN FIRE,
BURNING WHITE AND HOT.

On the back were etched in minuscule Pali script the names of three widows of kings who had sung as they mounted the funeral pyre after it had been set alight by this mirror in a Brahman's hand.

Next to the mirror lay a small lamp, also carved from rock crystal, bearing the sign of Vesta. It was intended to preserve the power of fire at hours without sun or at moments when haste was necessary. It was with this lamp, not with torches, that the funeral pyre near Olympus was lit the day Peregrine Proteus, later called Phoenix, leapt into the fire before an immense crowd in order to merge with the ether. The world knows of this man and his noble act only through Lucian's mendacious caricature.

Every good weapon contains magic; we are strengthened merely by the sight of it. So it was for us with Nigromontanus's mirror; its gleam prophesied that we would not perish completely, indeed, that base powers could not touch the best in us. Our higher powers remained invulnerable, as if secure in crystalline aeries.

Admittedly, Father Lampros would smile and say that there are also sarcophagi for the spirit. For him, the hour of annihilation was the hour of life. Of course, a priest fascinated by death as by a distant waterfall overhung with rainbows in its clouds of mist would speak this way. We, however, were in the prime of life and in great need of signs visible to the human eye. For us mortality appears only in the manifold colors of the one, invisible light.

17.

We noticed that the days when we were overcome by gloom were also days when fog rolled over the land, clouding its cheerful aspect. Mist billowed from the forests like steam from baleful kitchens and undulated in thick banks over the Campagna. It piled up against the Marble Cliffs and at daybreak flowed into the valley in sluggish streams, blanketing it in white haze up to the cathedral spires.

In this weather, we felt robbed of our eyesight and sensed evil creeping over the land as under a thick cloak. We did well to spend those days indoors with wine and light; and yet something often impelled us to venture outside. Not only did we have the feeling that the glowworms were up to their tricks out there but also that the land itself had been transformed—as if its very reality were waning. We frequently decided, therefore, to undertake expeditions on foggy days, most often seeking out the pasturelands. Our goal was always to acquire some particular plant. In the chaos we tried, if I may put it this way, to hold to Linnaeus's masterwork, which stands as one of those lookout towers from which the mind surveys tracts of wild growth. In this regard, a tiny plant can be a source of great illumination.

There was an additional aspect, which I would call shameful, and that is that we did not consider the forest scum our adversaries. We had resolved that we would engage only in hunting plants, not in battle, and therefore had to avoid roguery as one shuns swamps and wild animals. We did not attribute any freedom of will to these Lemures-rabble. Powers of this order must never be allowed to dictate the law to the point where we lose sight of the truth.

On those days, the steps leading to the top of the Marble Cliffs were damp from the fog, and chill winds whisked swaths of mist over them. Although the pasturelands were greatly changed, we still knew the old paths well. They led us through the ruins of wealthy farmsteads, now imbued with the smell of cold ashes. In the collapsed stables we saw the white bones, hooves, and horns of cattle, chains still around their necks. In the inner courtyards, there were piles of household goods that the glowworms had thrown from the windows as they plundered. A cradle lay in pieces between a chair and a table, the green of nettles rising around them. Only rarely did we encounter scattered bands of herdsmen, their beasts few and pitiful. Cadavers left to rot in the fields spread pestilence, wiping out much of the herds. The downfall of order brings good to none.

After an hour we came to old Belovar's farm, almost the only one that recalled the old times, since it stood untouched and rich with livestock in a wreath of green pastures. This was because Belovar was both a free herdsman and a clan chief. From the beginning of the troubles he had kept the roaming mobs from his property, so for a long time no hunter or glowworm dared pass through his lands, even at the edges. As for the rabble he slew in the fields or the undergrowth, he added them to his balance sheet of good deeds, not considering them worthy of new notches on his dagger. He was very strict in making sure that every dead animal bearing his brand was buried deep under a layer of lime to prevent foul air from spreading. So it was that one made one's way to him through large herds of pied and russet cattle, and the light from his home and barns shone far and wide. And the small idols that protected the borders of his land smiled and gleamed with fresh offerings.

An outer fort will sometimes remain intact in war long after the fortress has been sacked. As such, the old man's farmstead offered us a base camp. We could rest safely there and talk with him while in the kitchen his young wife, Milina, mulled saffron wine and set butter biscuits to bake. The old man's mother was still alive and even at one hundred she walked through the house and courtyard as upright as a candle. We liked speaking with the matriarch because she was very knowledgeable about herbs and knew incantations so powerful they made the blood run cold. We let her lay her hands on us as we bid them goodbye before continuing on our way.

Very often old Belovar wanted to accompany us, but we accepted his offer only reluctantly. His presence seemed to lure the forest rabble to us the way dogs become uneasy when a wolf enters their territory. That no doubt warmed the old man's heart; but we had other things on our minds. We went out without weapons or servants, clad in light, silver-gray cloaks to blend into the fog. We groped our way cautiously over moorland and reed fields towards the hornlike shrubs and the forest verge.

Soon after we left the pastures, we noticed that the violence was now closer and more menacing. The fog seethed in the boscage and the reed bed hissed in the wind. Yes, even the ground on which we walked seemed more alien and unfamiliar. Most disconcerting of all was our loss of memory. Then the land turned treacherous and variable, like terrain one sees in dreams. There were still some places we were certain we recognized but mysterious new tracts appeared right next to them like islands rising from the sea. Determining the true and accurate topography required all our powers of concentration, so we did well to avoid the adventures for which old Belovar thirsted.

We would walk and wander for hours in these moors and marshes. If I omit the details of this work it is because we did things there that lie outside the bounds of language and therefore elude the spell of words. Nevertheless, each of us remembers that his spirit, whether in dream or in profound thought, struggled in regions beyond description. It was like trying to feel one's way through a labyrinth or to discern the design of an optical illusion. And sometimes one's spirit wakes filled with wondrous strength. In such moments we did our best work. It also seemed that language did not suffice for the battle we were waging and that we would have to penetrate the very depths of dreams to confront the menace.

When we stood alone on moor and marsh, we truly had the sense that we were engaged in a subtle game in which every move provokes a countermove. Then the fog seethed more densely and at the same time the strength that can impose order seemed to grow within us.

18.

For all that, we never neglected the flowers on these forays. They indicated our direction as a compass shows the way over unknown waters. So it was that day too, when we ventured deep into the Flayer's Horn, a day we later remembered only with sheer horror.

That morning, when we saw fog billowing from the forests all the way to the Marble Cliffs, we decided to hunt for the red helleborine and set out promptly after Lampusa served us breakfast. The red helleborine is a rare orchid that blooms sparsely in forests and thickets. Linnaeus gave it the name *Serapias rubra* to distinguish it from two paler species; yet it blooms less frequently than these. Because this plant prefers areas where the thicket is less dense, Brother Otho suggested that Köppels-Bleek would the best place to hunt for it. This ancient clearing of ill repute, as the herdsmen called it, was said to be located where the forest verge gave onto the sickle of the Flayer's Horn.

At midday we stopped at old Belovar's, but because we felt we would need every ounce of our mental powers, we declined his offer of sustenance. We pulled on our silver-gray cloaks and after the matriarch had laid hands on us without our resistance, the old man sent us on our way reassured.

Just as we crossed his property line, we were engulfed in a roiling wave of fog that obscured all shapes and soon led us astray. So we wandered in circles over moor and heath, pausing now and again to rest between clusters of old willows or beside murky ponds in which tall rushes grew.

The wasteland seemed more alive that day, for we heard calls in the fog and believed we could make out figures in the mist gliding past very close to us although without seeing us. We would surely have lost the way to the Flayer's Horn in the confusion had we not tracked the sundews. We knew this small plant had colonized the belt of moist soil that ringed the forest and followed the pattern of its gleaming green, red-haired leaves like the fringe of a carpet. In this way, we reached the three tall poplars that in clear weather marked the tip of the Flayer's Horn like the shafts of three spears. From there we felt our way along the thicket's sickle-shaped arc to the edge of the forest and entered the horn at its widest point.

After pushing through a thick hem of blackthorn and cornelian cherry shrubs, we entered the high forest—never had the stroke of an axe rung through these depths. The ancient trunks, the Head Forester's pride, stood gleaming in the dampness like columns, their capitals hidden by the mist. We strode between them as through broad vestibules with tendrils of ivy and, like an enchanted stage set, flowering clematis dangled from invisible heights overhead. The ground was thick with humus and rotting branches, their bark covered with fiery scarlet cup fungi, and we felt like divers advancing through coral gardens. Where one of these enormous trunks had been felled by age or lightning, we stepped into a small clearing filled with thick clusters of yellow foxglove. Belladonna also grew profusely in the moldering ground and their sprays of brownish-violet calyxes trembled like funeral bells.

The air was still and oppressive and we scared away many kinds of birds. We heard the fine chirping with which the wood grouse streaks through the larches and the warning cry with which the startled thrush breaks off its songs. The wryneck hid, chuckling, in hollow alder trunks, and the orioles' fluttering laughter in the crowns of the oaks escorted us on our way. And in the distance, we heard cock pigeons cooing drunkenly and woodpeckers hammering dead wood.

We were advancing slowly along a low rise when Brother Otho, who was a short distance ahead of me, called back that we had almost reached the clearing. At that very moment, I caught sight of the orchid we were seeking shimmering in the gloom, and I joyfully rushed towards it. This flower resembled a little bird nestling beneath copper-colored foliage of the beech trees. I saw the slender leaves and the crimson flower with the pale pointed labellum that are its distinguishing traits.

The scholar, catching sight of a tiny plant or an animal by surprise, is filled with happiness as if nature had enriched him with great treasure. It was my habit, when I made such finds, to call Brother Otho over before I touched it so he could share my joy, but just as I was about to look in his direction, I heard a moan that filled me with horror. It was the sound of breath slowly leaving a chest after the body has suffered a terrible wound. I saw him standing spellbound on the top of the rise, and when I hurried over to him, he raised his hand to direct my gaze. I felt claws grip my heart—spread out before me lay a scene of oppression in all its ignominy.

19.

We stood behind a small bush filled with fiery red berries and looked down at the clearing of Köppels-Bleek. The weather had changed, for there was no trace of the trailing mist that had accompanied us from the Marble Cliffs. Things now stood out in sharp clarity as if in the calm, motionless air in the eye of a whirlwind. The birds, too, had fallen silent. Only a cuckoo fluttered here and there along the dark edge of the forest following the custom of its tribe. Now close by, now from a distance, we heard its mocking, quizzical laughter—

cuckoo, cuckoo—in a triumphantly increasing tempo that made our blood run cold. The clearing was overgrown with dried grass that gave way only on the far edge to the gray fuller's teasel one finds in scrapyards. In stark contrast to this arid space were two large, strangely fresh bushes that we took for laurels at first glance, but their leaves were covered with yellow spots like those seen in butcher shops. They grew on either side of an old barn that stood in the clearing with its doors wide open. The light illuminating it was not direct sunlight but, glaring and casting no shadows, it sharply defined the contours of the whitewashed building. The walls were divided in sections by dark beams supported on three feet and above them rose a pitched gray shingle roof. A variety of stakes and hooks were propped against the walls.

Over the dark, yawning doors a skull was affixed to the gable end; it bared its teeth in the ashen light and seemed to invite entry with its grin. Like a jewel on a necklace, the skull was the culmination of a narrow gable frieze that appeared to be made of brown spiders. But we immediately realized these were human hands fastened to the wall. We saw them so clearly that we could discern the small stakes driven through each of the palms.

The trees that lined the clearing, too, were hung with whitening skulls; some of these, their eye sockets already filling with moss, seemed to be observing us with dark smiles. All was silent save for the cuckoo's wild dance among the bleaching skulls. I heard Brother Otho murmur, half dreaming, "Yes, this is Köppels-Bleek."

The inside of the barn was almost pitch-black: all we could make out, near the entrance, was a flaying bench on which a skin was being stretched. Behind it pale, spongy masses shimmered against a dark background. We saw swarms of steel-colored and golden flies buzzing around them in the barn as in a hive. Then the shadow of a large bird fell over the clearing. It was cast by a vulture with jagged wings swooping down onto the teasel field. Only after we watched it slowly rooting with its beak in the dug-up earth all the way to its red neck did we notice that a dwarf was busy there with a mattock. The bird was following his work as ravens follow a plow.

The dwarf put down the mattock and headed towards the barn, whistling a tune. He wore a gray vest and we saw him rub his hands as if satisfied with his work. After he entered the barn, he began pounding and scraping on the flaying bench, whistling all the while in his demonic cheerfulness. Then we heard, as if in accompaniment, the wind sway through the thicket and the pale skulls hung on the trees rattled in chorus. Mingled with the rushing of the wind were the clattering of the hooks and the rustling of the desiccated hands against the barn wall. The knocking of wood and bone sounded like a puppet show in the kingdom of the dead. At the same time, a penetrating smell of decay, heavy and sweet, wafted towards us on the wind and chilled us to the marrow. We felt, in our innermost core, life's melody sound its deepest, darkest chord.

Later, we could not say how long we had looked on this specter—perhaps only for an instant. Then, as if waking from a dream, we grabbed each other by the hand and plunged back into the high forest of Flayer's Wood, pursued by the cuckoo's jeering cry. Now we knew the baleful kitchen from which the fog spread over the Marina—because we refused to give up, the old forester had shown it to us a bit more clearly. Such are the cellars over which the proud castles of tyranny rise and above which the aromas of their feast swirl:

putrid caves of a gruesome kind in which the depraved rabble regales itself with the violation of human dignity and liberty for all eternity. Then the muses fall silent and truth begins to flicker like a lamp in a foul wind. The weak give way when the fog has barely begun to brew and even the warrior caste hesitates when the Larvae-rabble climb up from the depths and onto the bastions. So it is that in this world the warrior's courage is in second place; only the very best among us penetrate to the seat of horror itself. They know that in truth all these images reside only in our hearts; they stride through them to victory's proud gates as through insubstantial reflections. Thus do these Larvae-rabble magnificently confirm their higher reality.

The dance of death on Köppels-Bleek, however, terrified us to the core and we stood shuddering deep in the woods, listening to the cuckoo's cry. Then shame gradually crept over us and it was Brother Otho who insisted we return to the clearing because the red helleborine was not registered in our field book. It was our custom, in fact, to enter every plant we found in a journal at the very time and place of discovery, for we had learned by experience that our memories are not reliable. We can, therefore, justifiably say that our *Florula Marinae* grew in the field.

So once again, without balking at the cuckoo's cry, we resumed our hunt along the low rise and searched for the little plant among the greenery. After we had examined it carefully again, Brother Otho dug up its rootstock with our trowel. We then measured every part of the plant with the compass and entered the date along with the location coordinates in our little notebook.

We humans fulfill an office when we work in our allotted professions—and it is strange how we are then filled with a powerful sense of invulnerability. We had already had this experience on the battlefield where the warrior happily turns to duties required by his rank when death's proximity threatens to sap his courage. Science had often shored up our strength in this way. There is great power that comes from looking at things consciously, eyes unclouded by any base obfuscations. The eye is nourished by the sight of creation in a particular way, and this alone is science's true power. And so Brother Otho and I could feel this ephemeral little flower, through its imperishable form and structure, giving us strength to withstand corruption's breath.

As we later made our way through the high forest to its edge, the sun came out again the way it sometimes does on foggy days just before it sets. A golden sheen filled the gaps in the enormous trees' crowns and the moss under our feet was gilded too. The cuckoo's cries had long since faded and invisible nightingales were gathered on the highest withered twigs, exquisite singers whose voices blended perfectly with the humid coolness of the air. Then evening descended with a green shimmer as if from verdant grottos. The garlands of honeysuckle hanging down from above gave off a rich scent and the colorful hawk moths rose, whirring, to their horned yellow flowers. We watched them perch on the lips of outstretched calyxes, trembling and as if lost in a voluptuous dream, then thrust their tremulous, slender, slightly bent proboscises into the honeyed recesses.

When we exited the Flayer's Horn near the three poplars, the moon's pale sickle had already begun to take on shades of gold and the stars shone in the firmament. Near the rush-filled pond we met old Belovar, who had set out in the twilight on our trail with his servants and trackers. The old man laughed when over saffron wine we showed him the red flower we had bagged in Köppels-Bleek; but we said no more and on parting urged him to guard his beautiful, unscathed farm carefully.

20.

There are experiences that force us to examine everything anew, and our glimpse of the flaying shed in Köppels-Bleek was one. We initially decided to seek out Father Lampros, but the catastrophe broke over us before we were able to visit the monastery of the Falcifera. We spent the following day sorting our manuscripts in the herbarium and the library and preparing many other notes for the fire. Afterwards I sat for a moment at the terrace railing in the garden as darkness fell, enjoying the flowers' perfume. The sun's warmth still lay on the beds, yet the first coolness of evening rose from the grasses along the riverbank and overpowered the smell of dust. Then the scent of the lunaria and the bright evening primrose cascaded down the Marble Cliffs and into the garden of the Rue-Herb Retreat. As some of the odors sank earthwards and others ascended, a subtler, more delicate aroma wafted through those heavy waves.

I followed this aroma and saw that a tall goldband lily from Zipangu had bloomed in the gloaming. There was still enough light to discern the flaming golden stripe and the brown speckles that magnificently adorned the petals. The pistil emerged from its white setting like the clapper of a bell in a circle of six slender stamens. They were dusted with brown powder like the finest opium extract and because they were still untouched by the moths, the delicate sheath in the center of the blossom glowed. I bent over the stamens and saw that their filaments trembled like a musical instrument of nature's devising, like a carillon which emitted not a stream of notes but a musky essence. It will forever remain a source of wonder how these delicate life-forms are animated by such passion.

As I was contemplating the lily, a thin blue ray of light flashed on the vineyard road below and groped its way over the slopes. Then I heard an automobile stop at the main gate. Although we were not expecting guests, I went down to the gate, hurrying because of the vipers, and there I saw a powerful car, humming softly like the almost imperceptible whirring of an insect. It bore the colors reserved to the high nobility of New Burgundy, and before it stood two men, one of whom made the sign with which Mauretanians identify themselves in the dark. He told me his name, Braquemart, one I recalled, and introduced the other as the young Prince of Sunmyra, a lord of New Burgundian lineage.

I invited them into the Rue-Herb Retreat and took them by the hand to lead them. Three abreast, we climbed the serpents' path in the faint light and I saw that the prince paid little attention to the creatures, whereas Braquemart sidestepped them scornfully but with great care.

We went into the library, where we met Brother Otho, and while Lampusa served wine and biscuits, we engaged our visitors in conversation. We knew Braquemart from earlier days but had only ever seen him briefly, because he was often traveling. He was a short, dark, gaunt fellow whom we found to be cut from a rather coarse cloth but, like all Mauretanians, he did not lack wit. He was one of those we jokingly called "tiger hunters" because we often met them embarked on some exotic adventure. He sought danger the way others climb richly crevassed massifs for sport: he despised the plains. Stronghearted, he did not shy away from obstacles; unfortunately, however, this virtue was paired with contempt. Like all zealots of power and supremacy, his wildest dreams were reserved to utopian realms. He believed there had always been two races on this earth—masters and slaves—and that over the course of time some interbreeding had occurred. In this regard, he was a disciple of old Petardier and, like the latter, called for them to be separated again. Like every crude theoretician, he fed on those sciences of the moment and was particularly occupied with archeology. He was not nuanced enough to suspect that our spades infallibly uncover the very evidence we already have in mind, and like many before him, he had in this way discovered the first cradle of the human race. We were present at the assembly when he reported on his excavations, and we heard how he had come upon a strange tableland in some distant desert. Tall columns of porphyry rose from the vast plain—they had withstood the weather's onslaughts and stood like bastions or rocky islands. Braquemart had scaled these columns and on their high plateaus he had found the ruins of princely palaces and temples of the sun he dated to prehistoric times. After he had described their dimensions and characteristics, he evoked a picture of the land. He portrayed lush, green prairies settled by herders and farmers with their flocks as far as the eye could see and, above them, perched on the porphyry columns and their red splendor, the aeries of this world's first rulers. He set ships with purple decks sailing down a river that had long since run dry; we could see the hundred oars dip into the water with insect-like regularity and hear the clash of cymbals and the crack of the whip that lashed the ill-fated galley slaves. These images were fitting for Braquemart. He was of that breed of men who dream concretely, a very dangerous sort.

The young prince also struck us as distant and distracted, but in a very different way. He could not have been much more than twenty, and yet the shadow of extreme suffering in his face stood in odd contrast to his age. Although tall, he stood with a pronounced stoop, as if his height caused him difficulties. He hardly seemed to hear what we were discussing. I had the impression that advanced age and extreme youth were united in him—the age of his lineage and the youth of his person. Decadence was thus deeply ingrained in his entire being; he bore the trait of ancestral greatness and the contrary feature the earth itself imprints on all heredity—for heredity is the wealth of the dead.

I had indeed expected, in the last stages of the struggle for the Marina, that the nobility would come forward—for a people's suffering burns hottest in noble hearts. When the sense of justice and tradition wanes and when terror clouds the mind, then the strength of the man in the street soon runs dry. Yet within the ancient aristocracy, the sense of what is true and legitimate abides and from these families new shoots of righteousness emerge. This is why noble blood is granted preeminence in all peoples. I had believed that one day armed men would rise up from the castles and fortresses as chivalrous leaders in the battle for freedom. Instead I saw before me this prematurely aged man, himself in need of support, whose appearance made perfectly clear how advanced the decline already was. And yet, it was astonishing that this languid dreamer felt called to offer protection to others—in this way the weakest and the purest assume the heavy burdens of this world.

At the front gate below, I had already had a sense of what

led these two men to us with dimmed lanterns, and my brother, Otho, too, seemed to know it before any word had been spoken. Then Braquemart asked us to give an account of the situation, which Brother Otho did in great detail. We gathered from the way Braquemart listened that he was extremely well informed about all the forces lined up against each other. He had already spoken to Biedenhorn; the only person he did not know was Father Lampros.

The prince, on the contrary, sat hunched in weary reverie. Even the mention of Köppels-Bleek, which put Braquemart in a good mood, seemed to pass him by; only when he heard about the profanation of the eburnum did he bolt from his seat in fury. Brother Otho then spoke in general terms about our opinion of things and what conduct we felt was appropriate. Braquemart listened politely but with an expression of ill-concealed scorn. We could read in his face that he considered us mere dreamers, ineffectual, and had soon passed judgment. There are situations in which each party deems the other a fantasist.

It may seem strange that Braquemart would want to oppose the Head Forester in this conflict even though many of their thoughts and actions were aligned. But we often make the mistake of conflating a similarity of means with a similarity of goals and a unity of motivations driving them. The difference was that the Head Forester intended to populate the Marina with wild beasts while Braquemart saw it as a land that would furnish slaves and captive armies. It was, fundamentally, an internal conflict among the Mauretanians, which is not feasible to elucidate here. Suffice it to say that there is a profound difference between fully formed nihilism and unchecked anarchy. The outcome of the struggle will determine whether human settlements will become wasteland or virgin forest. With regard to Braquemart, he was marked by all the traits of full-fledged nihilism. His was a cold, rootless intelligence with a penchant for utopias. He, like all his kind, saw life as the workings of a timepiece and so in his eyes violence and terror were simply the wheels that drive life's clock. At the same time, he indulged in the idea of a second, artificial nature and became intoxicated by scents of man-made flowers and the pleasures of a simulated sensuality. In his heart, creation had been suffocated and reconstructed like the mechanism of a toy. Frost flowers bloomed on his forehead. On seeing him, one inevitably thought of his master's profound saying: "The desert grows—woe to him who carries deserts within!"

Nevertheless, we still felt some sympathy for Braquemart—not so much because he was fearless, for the closer to stone a man is, the less credit he deserves for bravery. Rather, we were drawn by a subtle suffering—the bitterness of a man who had lost all hope of salvation. For this he sought vengeance on the world, the way a child destroys a bed of flowers in futile rage. He did not spare himself and penetrated the labyrinths of terror with cold audacity. Similarly, when we lose the sense of our fatherland, we set out in search of distant worlds filled with adventure.

Braquemart modeled his thinking on life and insisted that ideas be armed, tooth and claw. Yet his theories were like distillations without any real vitality; they lacked the delicious element of lavishness that gives any dish its flavor. His projects all suffered from aridity even though not a single flaw could be found in his logic; so a bell's sonority is sapped by an invisible fault. This was due to the fact that for him, power was expressed too much in thought and not enough in grandezza, or in innate disinvolture. In this respect, he could not match the Head Forester, who wore his power like an old hunting jacket that fit more comfortably the more it was soaked with dirt and blood. For this reason, too, I had the sense that Braquemart was about to embark on an ill-fated adventure; in such encounters the theorist is never a match for the pragmatist.

Braquemart was no doubt aware of his weakness compared to the Head Forester and that was why he had brought along the young prince. The prince, however, seemed to us to be following an entirely different set of motivations; in such situations, surprising alliances are often formed. Perhaps the prince was using Braquemart the way one uses a boat to make a crossing. That frail body contained a powerful impulse towards suffering and he steered towards it as in a dream, thoughtlessly but with assurance, just as on the battlefield the best soldiers, even in the throes of death, will rise from the ground when they hear the bugle call to attack.

Later, Brother Otho and I often thought back to this conversation presided over by a baleful star. The prince scarcely uttered a word and Braquemart displayed the impatient superiority that marks the technician. He was clearly inwardly amused by our misgivings. Without letting slip a single word about his plans, he asked about the position of the pasture-land and the forest. He was also eager for details about Fortunio's adventures and demise. From his questions we could see that he intended to explore the region or even begin operations there and we had a foreboding that, like a bad doctor, he would aggravate the malady. After all, it was not a coincidence nor any adventure that had the old forester and his Lemures-rabble emerging from the forest depths and beginning their activity. Before, riffraff of this kind were dealt with like thieves, and their now swelling ranks indicated profound disruptions in the order and health of the people, indeed, in their fortunes as a whole. Intervention was sorely needed and this required marshals to restore order and new theologians able to see the evil clearly, from its external manifestations down to its finest roots; only then would it be time for the consecrated sword to strike a blow that would rend the darkness like a bolt of lightning. Accordingly, it was incumbent on each individual to enter more clearly and intentionally into ties with others and garner a new trove of legitimacy. One lives by special rules to win a race, even a short one. But in this case the highest form of life, freedom and human dignity itself, were at stake. Braquemart, it is true, held such considerations to be rank foolishness and intended to pay the Head Forester back in kind. He had lost his self-respect and that loss is the source of all human ills.

We discussed this subject at great length. Even when we could not understand each other through words, our silences were eloquent. Minds confer before a decision like doctors around a sick man's bed. One recommends the knife, another wants to spare the patient, and a third weighs a special remedy. But what good are counsel and determination when downfall is already written in the stars? Even so, war councils are convened on the eve of lost battles.

The prince and Braquemart intended to set out for the pasturelands that very night and because they refused to let us guide or accompany them, we recommended they take old Belovar. Then we escorted them to the stairs on the Marble Cliffs. We formally bid them farewell as is done after an encounter without warmth or profit. Yet our leave-taking was followed by a silent scene that left me disconcerted. Both men paused in the twilight on the cliffs and observed us in silence for a long time. The cool morning air had begun

to rise, in which for a brief moment the eye sees things un-
fold as if reborn, new and mysterious. And so did we perceive
the prince and Braquemart. It seemed to me that Braquemart's
face had lost its superior smirk and now bore a human smile.
The young prince, on the other hand, now stood upright
and looked at us serenely—as if he knew the answer to a
puzzle that confounded us. We remained silent for a long
time, then Brother Otho took the prince's hand one last
time and bowed deeply over it.

After we lost sight of the pair behind the edge of the
Marble Cliffs, I sought out the goldband lily for a moment
before I lay down to rest. The slender dust vessels had been
beaten by insect wings and the golden-green depths of the
calyxes were spotted with crimson powder. The large moths
had no doubt scattered it during their nuptial feast.

So do honey and bitterness flow from every hour. And as
I bent over the dewy chalices, the first cry of the cuckoo
sounded from the distant forest verge.

21.

We spent the morning in a state of worry because the automobile stood abandoned at our gate. At breakfast, Lampusa
handed us a note from Phyllobius that made it clear the visit
had not gone unnoticed. He requested that we urge the
prince to visit him at the monastery; Lampusa had been
woefully negligent in delivering his request.

At noon, old Belovar arrived to announce that the young
prince and Braquemart had appeared at his farm at dawn.
Studying a painted piece of parchment, Braquemart asked

him about various points in the forests. Then the two men set off again and old Belovar sent scouts after them. The two had entered the forest in the stretch between the Flayer's Horn and the copse with the red steer.

From this news we knew we could expect evil tidings and wished the two men had set out with a few of Belovar's sons and farmhands as had been offered. We knew Braquemart's central tenet that no one is more formidable than persons of distinction, and we thought it possible that the two would seek out the bloodthirsty old leader himself and confront him in his inner courtyard. But they were soon caught in the nets of demonic powers—we suspected that Lampusa's delay was tied to these nets. We thought of Fortunio's fate, a man of many gifts who had studied the forests closely before he ventured into them. It was no doubt his map that had ended up in Braquemart's possession after many a detour. After Fortunio's death we had searched far and wide for his map and eventually learned that it had fallen into the hands of treasure hunters.

The pair had walked into danger unprepared and without any superior guidance, like simple adventure-seekers. They went like half-men—here, Braquemart, pure technician of power, who only ever saw parts of things and never their roots; and there, Prince Sunmyra, a noble spirit who was acquainted with order and justice but was like a child venturing into forests where wolves howl. Nonetheless, we believed Father Lampros could have profoundly changed and united them, as can be effected through the intercession of mysteries. We wrote a note informing him of the situation and sent Erio in haste to the monastery of the Falcifera.

We had felt uneasy ever since the prince and Braquemart had appeared at our retreat, yet we now saw things more clearly than before. We sensed they were coming to a head and that we would have to swim through them as through swirling currents in a narrow passage. We also deemed the time had come to prepare the mirror of Nigromontanus and we wanted to kindle the light while the sun remained propitious. We ascended to the inner gallery and, according to the rites, lit the flame from the celestial fire through the crystal disc. With great joy we watched the blue flame descend, then we hid the mirror and lamp in the niche that held the household gods.

We were still changing our clothes when Erio returned with the monk's answer. He had found Father Lampros at prayer and he had immediately handed the boy a letter without reading our note. Thus are long-prepared sealed orders dispatched.

For the first time we saw the letter was signed Lampros and adorned with his crest and his motto: PATIENCE IS MINE. For the first time, too, there was no mention of plants. Instead, the monk asked me in few words to follow the prince and watch over him, and he advised me not to go unarmed.

It was important that I equip myself with great dispatch and, hastily exchanging a few sentences with Brother Otho, I donned my old, tried-and-tested hunting jacket that had withstood the test of every thorn. The Rue-Herb Retreat, truth be told, was ill-equipped in weaponry. Over the chimney hung an old shotgun, the kind used for duck hunting, but with a shortened barrel. We had used it now and again on our travels to shoot at reptiles whose thick skin and hard life make them better felled by a hail of buckshot than the surest rifle shot. The sight of the gun brought to mind the musky scent that greets the hunter in the sultry riverside thicket as he approaches the places the large saurians come ashore. For those hours when land and water merge in the twilight, we would attach a silver front sight to the barrel. This was the only device in our house we could call a weapon; that is why I took it, and Brother Otho fitted me with the large leather hunting bag that had nooses on the front flap to hang shot birds and an inside strap for shells.

So in haste do we grab the first thing at hand; and Father Lampros had no doubt advised me to carry a weapon more as a sign of liberty and hostility, the way we bring flowers when visiting a friend. The good sword I had worn with the Purple Riders hung in my father's house far to the north; still, I never would have chosen it for such an expedition. It had flashed in the sun in the midst of heated cavalry battles when the ground thundered with hoofbeats and our chests would swell gloriously. I had drawn it as we advanced at an easy, rocking gallop that set our weapons rattling, lightly at first, then ever louder, and we each turned our sights on a particular adversary in the enemy squadron. And I had relied on it in those moments of single combat when through the tumult we glimpse the wide-open plain and many bare saddles. More than a few blows had fallen on the guards of Franconian rapiers and on the basket hilts of Scottish sabers—and under other blows, the wrists had felt the vulnerability of exposure as the blade cut them to the quick. Yet all these combatants, even the free sons of the barbarian tribes, were noble men who presented their chests to the steel for the sake of their fatherland; and at banquets we could have raised a glass to each as to a brother. In battle the valiant of this world establish the limits of freedom; and weapons drawn against them are not to be used on butchers and bullies. I hurriedly took leave of Brother Otho and of Erio. It seemed a good omen that the boy looked at me with cheerful confidence. Then I set off accompanied by the old herdsman.

22.

Dusk was falling when we reached the large farm in the pastureland. We saw from a distance that the place was in an uproar; the stalls glowed in the light of torches and echoed with the bellows of the cattle that were being rashly rounded up. The herdsmen we met were armed, and they told us that others were still out in remote parts of the Campagna where livestock had to be protected. We were greeted in the court-yard by Belovar's eldest son, Sombor, a giant of a man with a full red beard, holding a whip threaded with iron beads. He reported that unrest had broken out in the forests at midday; they had seen smoke rising and heard a commotion. Then droves of glowworms and hunters had emerged from the marshy thickets along the Flayer's Horn and driven off a herd grazing on an outlying pasture. Sombor had retrieved a part of their plunder on the marshland, but to judge by the troops of foresters he saw, they could expect a sally of some kind. In the meantime, his scouts had spotted patrols and lone men in other locations, such as the copse with the red steer, and even at our backs. Good fortune had led us to the farm just before we would have been cut off.

Given this state of affairs, I could hardly expect Belovar to accompany me on my venture into the forests, and I thought it proper for him to concern himself with his prop-erty and his people. But I did not yet truly know the old fighter or the zeal he was capable of showing for his friends.

He immediately vowed that house and barn and stalls could burn to the ground before he would let me take a single step alone in these times, and he entrusted his son Sombor with safeguarding the farm. At these words, the women who were hauling valuables out of the house quickly knocked on wood and crowded around us, wailing. Then the matriarch approached and laid hands on us from head to toe. On my right shoulder, her fingers halted in concern, but on the second pass, they slid freely. But when she touched her son's forehead, she was seized with terror and covered her face with her hands. At this, the young woman threw herself at the old man's chest with a shrill cry like the lamentations heard at funerals.

The old man was impervious to women's tears, all the more so when the intoxication of battle was coursing in his veins. He cleared a space with both his arms, like a swimmer parting the waves, and in a loud voice summoned his sons and farmhands by name. He selected only one patrol and left the rest to help his son Sombor guard the farm. For the patrol he chose only those who had already killed a man in the clan wars, the ones he called his cockerels when in good humor. They came with leather jerkins and leather hoods, bearing the crude weapons that had been stored in the armories of the pastureland farms for generation after generation. The torches' glow illuminated halberds and spiked maces and thick staffs on which sharp axe-heads and saw-toothed spears were mounted, as well as pikes, grappling irons, and an array of hooks. With these old Belovar intended to clear out and sweep away the forest rabble to his heart's content.

Then the kennel boys opened the doors behind which the packs barked and howled—the sleek hounds and the sturdy mastiffs, some baying high and clear, others hoarsely. They shot forward and filled the courtyard, panting and growling, behind the massive lead dog, Leontodon. He leapt up to Belovar and, whining, put his paws on the old man's shoulders, giant that he was. The kennel boys gave them copious water to drink and poured a basin of blood from the slaughter onto the stone floor for them to lap up.

These two packs were the old man's pride and it was surely in great part because of them that the forest rabble had kept clear of his farm in those years. For his light pack he had bred the fleet Arabian hound that shares the nomad's sleeping rugs and whose pups the nomad's young wife suckles at her breast. Every twitch in these sight hounds' bodies was as visible as if an anatomist had exposed their very muscles and motion was such a force in them that constant tremors ran over their bodies even as they dreamt. Of all the swift animals on this earth, only cheetahs can outrace them, and only over a short distance at that. They hunted in pairs, cutting off the quarry's attempted evasions and clamping their jaws tight on its shoulders. Yet some hunted alone, taking their victims by the throat and holding fast until the hunter arrived.

For his heavy pack old Belovar bred Molossian hounds, magnificent tawny beasts brindled with black. The breed's characteristic fearlessness was heightened by their having been crossbred with Tibetan mastiffs, which the Romans had set on aurochs and lions in the arena. The effects of the crossbreeding manifested itself in the dogs' size, proud bearing, and tails carried high like a standard. Almost all these guard dogs had deep scars in their coats—souvenirs of blows received from bears' paws on hunts. When leaving the woods for the pastures, the giant bear had to hug the forest's edge, because if the pack closed in around him, they would tear the beast to shreds before the hunters had time to finish him off.

The inner courtyard was filled with writhing, growling, and gulping; terrifying teeth gleamed in red maws. Added to this were the flickering torches, the rattling weapons, and the lamentations of the women fluttering around the farm like frightened pigeons. Old Belovar delighted in the commotion, complacently stroking his beard with his right hand and making his dagger dance in his red cloth belt with his left. He also carried a heavy double axe on a strap around his wrist.

Then the kennel boys, their arms covered with leather gauntlets to the shoulder, lunged at the dogs and bound them in pairs with leashes the color of coral. After that, we extinguished our torches and passed through the gates, headed towards the forest on the far side of the boundary markers.

The moon had risen and in its light I abandoned myself to those thoughts that steal upon us when we plunge into uncertainty. Memories arose in me of glorious morning hours when we rode in the vanguard ahead of our troops as the chorus of the young cavalry soldiers rang out behind us in the cool dawn. We felt our hearts beating solemnly and all the treasures of the world would have seemed meager next to the imminent pleasure of incisive and honorable action. Oh, what a difference there was between those hours and that night, when I saw weapons that resembled the claws and horns of some monster glittering in the pale moonlight. We entered the Lemures Forest, a place devoid of justice and of laws, where no fame can be won. And I experienced the vanity of all glory and honor along with profound bitterness.

Yet it was some consolation that, unlike the first time I had gone in search of Fortunio, I was not in thrall to some magical adventure but, summoned by a higher spiritual force, was following an upright cause. And I resolved not to cede to fear or to arrogance.

23.

Not far from the farm, we split up for the advance. We sent scouts ahead and had them follow the pairs of tracking dogs while the main patrol brought up the rear with the hounds. The moon was so bright you could read by its light, and as long as we were crossing the pastures, the various groups kept each other in sight. To our left we saw the three tall poplars like black lances and before us the dark mass of the Flayer's Horn, so it was easy to keep our bearings. We approached the arc of the forest where the sickle of the Flayer's Horn protruded from the woods.

I was positioned next to the old avenger with the light pack and facing the tip of the sickle. When the dogs reached the belt of reeds and alders that bordered the moor, we saw them stop short before plunging through a gap. As soon as they disappeared from our sight, we heard the nasty, whirring snap of iron jaws and a cry of agony. The scouts bolted back out of the undergrowth into the fields as we rushed forwards to intercept them and find out what had happened.

We saw that the gap through which the scouts had penetrated was overgrown with knee-high gorse and heather. It glowed in the moonlight and in its center a terrible spectacle met our eyes. We saw one of the young kennel boys suspended in the massive jaws of an iron snare like trapped game. His feet barely brushed the ground and his head and arms dangled backwards in the undergrowth. We rushed up to him and saw that he had been caught in a booby trap—as the old man called the large metal mantraps he had his men conceal on the forest footpaths. The sharp edge of the jaws had sliced into his chest and it was clear at a glance that he was beyond saving. Still, working together we forced open the spring trap to free the corpse from its embrace. In doing so we discovered that the trap was lined, like the jaws of a shark, with razor-edged teeth of blue steel, and once we had laid the dead man's body on the heather, we cautiously closed them again.

We assumed, of course, that lookouts were watching the trap, and in fact we heard a rustling in the bushes nearby as we stood silently around the victim of this vile weapon, and then a loud, mocking peal of laughter rang out in the night. At that, a stirring began to spread through the moor, as when crows have been disturbed in their roost. The sound of breaking branches and things being dragged spread through the pine stand and there was rustling along the dark trenches where the Head Forester had his duck-hunting blinds. At the same time, whistles and coarse voices echoed through the moor as if it were swarming with rats. We heard the mob growing bold, the way they bolster their courage in the slime of gutters and dungeons when they are sure they are in the majority. Indeed, they seemed to far outnumber us, for we heard the fraternities of rogues singing their obscene songs near and far. The La Picousière gang's song rang out very close to us. They stamped through the moor, croaking like toads:

> *Catherine a le craque moisi,*
> *Des seins pendants,*
> *Des pieds de cochon,*
> *La faridondaine.*

And the tall tufts of broom, the reeds, and willow bushes echoed in response. In this commotion we saw greenish will-o'-the-wisps flickering over the ponds and the waterfowl rose in startled flight.

Meanwhile the rest of our troop, with the heavy pack, had reached us at a run, and we noticed the kennel boys hesitate at the sight of these apparitions. Then old Belovar raised his booming voice:

"Forward, lads, forward! These blackguards are losing ground. But keep a sharp eye out for those traps!"

Without a backward glance he set off, the blades of his double axe glinting in the moonlight. The boys followed close behind, eager to get their hands on the trap setters. In small groups, we pushed our way through reeds and bushes, testing the ground the best we could. We sought passages between ponds on whose dark mirrors water lilies glowed and crept through the withered bulrushes with cotton wool fluffing from their dark spindles. We soon heard voices close by and felt the whoosh of shots graze our temples. Then the kennel boys set to riling the dogs until their fur bristled and their eyes flashed like burning embers. They released the dogs and like pale arrows they shot through the dark undergrowth whining happily.

Old Belovar was right when he had said the rabble would not dare defy us—as soon as the dogs attacked, cries of pain bolted out of the undergrowth followed by the baying of the pack hot on their traces. We charged after them and saw that a peat bog as flat as a barn floor lay on the far side of the scrub. The mob had fled to this expanse and were running for their lives to the high forest nearby. Only those spared by the dogs could reach it. We saw many of the rabble set upon by the dogs and forced to surrender—like pale flames in the empire of the damned, the animals circled the men and leapt at them ravenously. And here and there a fugitive had fallen and lay on the ground as if paralyzed, his neck in the jaws of a growling dog.

Then the kennel boys unleashed the heavy pack and the hounds stormed howling into the night. We saw how they felled their victims with a single bound and tore the quarry they fought over to pieces. The boys followed them and meted out the coup de grâce. Here there was no mercy, as in hell. They bent over the dead and threw the dogs their rewards. They had great difficulty leashing the dogs again.

We stood on the bog as if on the threshold of the dark forest. Old Belovar was in good spirits; he praised the kennel boys and dogs for their work and passed around strong drink. Then he pressed for a fresh attack before the forest rose up in riot because of the escaped rabble, and with his axe he breached the thick hedge that lined the forest. We were not far from the spot Brother Otho and I had entered in search of the red helleborine, and we would begin by attacking Klöppels-Bleek.

Soon the breach was as wide as a barn door. We lit our torches and stepped as if through a dark maw into the forest.

24.

Tree trunks gleamed like red pillars in the light of flames; smoke rose from our torches in thin, vertical threads that twined together high above us into a baldachin in the still air. We advanced in a broad line that narrowed to pass fallen trees and immediately spread out again. Still bearing our torches, we kept each other well in sight. To be sure of the way, the old man had brought along bags of chalk to mark our path with a light trail. That way he could be sure we would have a way to escape.

The dogs pulled in the direction of Klöppels-Bleek, drawn as always by the scent of hell and killing fields. Following their lead, we swiftly gained ground and easily moved ahead of the rest. Only now and then would a bird rise, beating its wings heavily, from some nest hidden in the treetops. And swarms of bats circled silently in the light of our torches.

Before long I believed I recognized the hill with the clearing; the rise glowed in the dull reflection of a fire. We stopped and again the voices reached us, but not as ostentatiously as earlier in the bog. Divisions of foresters seemed to be securing the woods and Belovar intended to clear them out as he had the bands of rogues. He had the tracker dogs brought to the fore, arranged them in a single line as if for a race, then released them into the night like bright projectiles. As the dogs sped, panting, through the undergrowth, we heard whistles from over there and a howling set in as if the savage hunter himself had appeared to receive them. They had run straight into the pack of mastiffs the Head Forester kept in his kennels.

Fortunio had told me about these vicious dogs, about their ferocity and strength, which were legendary. The Head Forester had bred them from the Cuban mastiff known for its red color and black mask. In earlier times the Spanish had trained these dogs to maul Indians and had shipped them to all the countries that had slaves and slaveholders. With their help, blacks in Jamaica were subdued again after rising victoriously in armed rebellion. The rebels, who had scorned iron and fire, surrendered as soon as the slave hunters disembarked with the braces of dogs, so terrifying was their appearance. The leader of the red pack was Chiffon Rouge, prized by the Head Forester for its direct blood line to the mastiff Becerrillo, whose name is fatally bound to the conquest of Cuba. It is said that Becerrillo's master, Captain Iago de Senazda, would sic the beast on captive Indian women for the delight of his guests. Again and again, such points in human history recur when humanity threatens to fall completely under the sway of the demonic.

From the horrifying cries, we knew our light pack was lost before we could send help. They must have been all the more quickly annihilated since they were of that pure race that will fight to the death rather than retreat. The red dogs bayed, and we heard them attack, their howling stifled as jaws closed greedily on fur and flesh, while the high, clear barks of the Arabian hounds died away in whimpers.

Old Belovar, seeing his noble creatures sacrificed in the blink of an eye, began to rage and curse, yet he did not dare send in his Molossian hounds, for these remained our strongest card in this uncertain round. So he called on his men to get ready and they rubbed the chests and jowls of the large animals with henbane brandy and fastened spiked collars around their necks for protection. Others propped their torches up against dead branches to prepare for the battle.

They were ready in no time at all and we had barely taken up position when the red pack broke over us like a thunderstorm. We heard them crashing through the dark undergrowth; then the ferocious beasts leapt into the area illuminated by the torches' ember glow. Chiffon Rouge led the charge, his neck encircled with a glinting fan of sharp blades. His held his head lowered and let his tongue loll, drooling, to the ground; his eyes looked up at us deviously. From a distance we could see his bared fangs glinting, the lower pair protruding tusklike from his jowls. Despite his great mass, the monster leapt forward in graceful bounds—in an oblique, dancing flight, as if in his overabundance of strength, he disdained to run straight at us. And behind him, marked in black and red, the entire bloodhound pack appeared in the torchlight.

Cries of fear rose at the sight and calls for the Molossians rang out. I saw old Belovar look at his dogs with worry, but the proud animals pulled at their leashes undaunted, eyes fixed straight ahead and ears erect. The old man glanced at me with a laugh and gave the signal. Like arrows shot from tightly drawn bows, the tawny hounds flew at the red pack. Leading the charge, Leontodon leapt at Chiffon Rouge.

In the red light under the giant trunks, howling and exultation broke out, as if an army of demons was passing by, and boiling bloodlust flooded the forest. Animals rolled over the ground in dark masses, tearing at each other's flesh; others gave chase around us in a wide circle. We tried to intervene in the carnage, the din of which filled the air, but it was difficult to strike the red mastiffs with blade or bullet without also wounding our Molossians. Only where the hunt spun around us as on a circular track was it possible to target them separately and bring them down, like shooting at birds in flight. It became clear that I had by chance made the best possible choice of a weapon in taking my shotgun. When aiming, I waited until I could see the black mask in my silver front sight, then I was sure my shot would fell the beast immediately without a single twitch.

But over there, too, on the other side, we saw guns flash and guessed that in the circular chase they were shooting our Molossians. In this sense the skirmish resembled an ellipse around two points of fire with the two packs battling along the short axis. While the fight raged, the track became illuminated with fiery columns as the torches fell and the dry underbrush burst into flame.

Soon it was clear that the Molossians outmatched the mastiffs, if not in strength of their bite then in their mass and power of attack. And yet, the red hounds outnumbered ours. It also appeared that fresh reinforcements were being thrown into the fray, because it became ever harder for us to assist our dogs. The bloodhounds were carefully trained to attack human beings, who were the Head Forester's favorite prey; and once the Molossian hounds were too few in number, fear for our own safety took our attention away from the animals' fight. Suddenly the red beasts began leaping at us, now from the dark bushes, now out of the smoke of the fires, their attacks heralded with screams. They lunged and we had to act quickly to stop them midair; some were pierced only at the last minute by the boys' spikes while old Belovar's double axe whistled down on others already stretched out on their victims, panting for the man's blood.

We soon perceived the first terrible cracks in our front; to me it seemed that the cries of Belovar's men became more vehement and more frantic—in such cases an undertone of stifled weeping signals that despair is about to get the upper hand. Those cries mingled with the howling of the pack, the bangs of gunshots, and the crackling of the flames. And from the trees we heard a peal of laughter ring, a roaring guffaw that announced the Head Forester had joined the fray. A terrible mirth, characteristic of him, resounded in this laughter; this old man was one of those great lords who exult when they are defied. Terror was his element.

Surrounded by this turmoil I grew heated; I could feel the excitement taking hold of me. Then, as often in the midst of combat, the image of my old fencing master, van Kerkhoven, flashed before me. A short Flemish man with a red beard who trained me in footwork, he often said that a well-aimed shot is better than ten fired hastily on the run. And he taught me that, when terror spreads in battle, one must keep the index finger extended and take deep, calm breaths—for he is strongest who breathes well.

Kerkhoven appeared before me—and indeed all true teaching is a spiritual matter and the image of an excellent teacher helps us weather distress. And just as when I faced targets on the shooting range up north, I paused, breathing slowly and deeply. I instantly felt my vision sharpen and my chest lighten.

The battle was taking a bad turn, and most perilous of all, smoke increasingly obscured our field of fire. The combatants were isolated; objects became indistinct. And the red dogs attacked us from ever closer. More than once I saw Chiffon Rouge pass near me, but no sooner did I have in him in my sights than the cunning beast found cover. I was flooded with a hunter's fury and, when I saw the dog disappear into the smoke flowing before me like a wide stream, my zeal to slay the Head Forester's favorite hound drove me to leap in after him.

25.

In the dense smoke I thought I glimpsed that shadowy monster now and again but always too fleetingly to aim and shoot. Mirages in the swirling haze fooled me; I finally stopped, uncertain of my bearings, and stood listening. Then I heard branches cracking and thought the beast might have circled back to attack me from behind. To protect myself, I knelt with a thornbush as cover for my back and held my shotgun raised.

In such circumstances, our eye is often caught by small details, and next to where I knelt I spotted a flower blooming in the withered leaves and recognized our red helleborine. I deduced from this that I was at the very place Brother Otho and I had entered the forest and therefore not far from the hilltop by Klöppels-Bleek. And, in fact, it took me only a few strides to reach the low summit that rose like an island from the smoke.

From the ridge I saw the clearing of Klöppels-Bleek bathed in a dull light and yet my glance was drawn to a fire burning deep in the forest. There I saw, as if drawn in red filigree, a tiny, crenellated castle with round towers consumed in flames, and I remembered that on Fortunio's map this spot was designated the "southern residence." The conflagration revealed that the prince and Braquemart's raid had reached the castle steps. As always when we witness the effects of bold action, a feeling of elation filled my breast. At the same time, I recalled the Head Forester's triumphant laughter and quickly turned my gaze to Klöppels-Bleek. The depravity I saw there made my blood run cold.

The fires that lit up Klöppels-Bleek were still burning hot, but now a thin layer of white ash covered them, like a silver dome. Their glimmer fell on the flaying shed, which stood wide open, and a red light bathed the skull grinning on the gable. From the footprints that covered the earth around the fires and traces in the vile lair, which I will not describe, it was clear that the Lemures had held one of their gruesome celebrations and the area was tinged in its afterglow. We humans look on such horrific visions with bated breath and as if through narrow cracks.

Suffice it to say that among all the old skulls, long stripped of flesh, I caught sight of two new ones, displayed on tall poles—the heads of the prince and Braquemart. High up on iron spikes with curving hooks, they looked down at the pallid flakes of ash rising from the inferno below. The prince's hair had gone white, but I found his features even nobler than before, imbued with that supreme, sublime beauty that suffering alone produces.

At the sight my eyes welled with tears—the kind of tears that fill us with a glorious exaltation as well as sorrow. I saw the shadow of an extraordinarily gentle, joyful smile playing on this ashen mask, from which the flayed skin hung in tatters, looking down onto the fire from atop the stake, and I recognized that step by step this noble man had shed his flaws the way a king drops the rags which disguised him as a beggar. A shudder ran through my core: I realized that the prince was worthy of his ancestors, slayers of monsters; he had vanquished the dragon fear in his breast. I had often doubted; now I was convinced: there were still noble beings among us in whose hearts knowledge of the higher order was preserved and perpetuated. A lofty example enjoins us to follow, and I swore before this head that for all the future I would cast my lot with the solitary and free rather than with the triumphant and servile.

Braquemart's features, on the other hand, were unchanged. From his stake he gazed down on Klöppels-Bleek with an air of mockery and faint disgust, constrained in the manner of a man who suffers a violent paroxysm but refuses to let it show. I would not have been surprised to have seen him wearing his usual monocle. His hair was still black and gleaming, and I surmised that he had swallowed in time the pill every Mauretanian always carries on him. It is a capsule of colored glass, most often hidden in a ring and, in moments of danger, in the mouth. One bite is enough to crush the capsule that contains a poison of rare toxicity. In the Mauretanian language, this is referred to as the appeal to the third authority—in accordance with the degree of violence and the concept of human dignity they foster in the Order. They consider their dignity compromised by any dishonorable violence and all Mauretanians are expected to be prepared at any moment for the deadly summons. This, then, was Braquemart's final adventure.

Stupefied, I took in this spectacle, and I do not know how long I stood observing it, as if outside of time. Meanwhile, I fell into a waking dream, forgetful of the proximity of danger. In this state we sleepwalk through perils—without caution but still attuned to the spirit of things. And so I stepped into the Klöppels-Bleek clearing and, as when one is intoxicated, things appeared distinct and yet they were not outside me. They were as familiar to me as in the enchanted realm of childhood; all around me the white skulls on the old trees looked at me inquiringly. I heard shots whistling through the clearing along with the low vibration of crossbow bolts and the sharp cracks of rifle shots. They passed so close to me that they ruffled the hair at my temples, but for me they were simply a deep accompanying melody that set the tempo of my steps.

In the light of the silvery embers, I walked up to the abominable site and pulled down the pole on which the prince's head was impaled. With both hands, I lifted his head from the iron spike and placed it gently in my leather game bag. While I knelt to accomplish this task, I felt a violent blow to my shoulder. One of the shots must have hit me, but I felt no pain, nor did I see any blood on my leather jerkin. Still, my right arm dangled paralyzed. As if woken from sleep, I looked around and rushed back into the forest with the exalted trophy. I had left my rifle next to the red helleborine, and in any case it was no further use to me. I immediately hastened back to the place I had left the combatants.

Silence had fallen over the battle site; the torches had burned out. Only where the bushes had caught fire was there still a faint red glow. In this dim light, the eye could make out the corpses of fighters and dogs on the dark ground; they were horribly maimed and mauled. In their midst, Belovar was lying propped against the trunk of an old oak tree. His head was split open and the stream of blood had colored his white beard. The double axe at his side and the broad dagger still clutched in his right hand were also red with blood. At his feet lay the faithful Leontodon, his skin torn to shreds by gunshots and knife blades, licking his master's hand as he died. The old man had fought well, for around him lay a wreath of men and dogs he had mown down. He had found a fitting death in the thick of the chase, when red hunters pursue red game through the forests, and death and sensuality are intertwined. I looked deep into my dead friend's eyes, and with my left hand, I placed a fistful of earth on his chest. He had celebrated at the wild, sanguinary feasts of the Great Mother, and she is proud of such sons.

26.

To find my way out of the dark forest and back to the pasturelands I had only to follow the chalk traces we had left on our advance. Deep in thought I walked along the white path.

It seemed strange to me that during the carnage I had found myself with the dead, and I saw this as a symbol. I remained lost in reverie. This state was not entirely new to me; I had experienced it before at the close of days in which I had had a brush with death. At such times, through the power of our minds, we can escape our bodies somewhat and, as it were, walk as a companion at the side of our own image. But I had never yet felt the loosening of these slender ties as distinctly as there in the forest. I followed the white track dreamily and saw the world around me as in the dark gleam of an ebony forest in which small ivory figures were reflected. In this state, I crossed the moor at Flayer's Horn and entered the Campagna not far from the three tall poplars.

Here I saw to my horror that the sky was ominously lit by conflagrations. An evil commotion filled the pasturelands and shadows rushed past me. Farmhands who had escaped the slaughter may have been there, but I did not call to them: many seemed drunk with rage. Some swung firebrands, and I heard men speaking La Picousière slang. Crowds of them laden with booty were hurrying back to the forest. The copse of the red steer was brightly lit; from it came women's screams mingled with the bursts of laughter of a victory feast.

Filled with dark apprehension, I hurried to the farmstead. Even from a distance I could see that Sombor and his men had succumbed to the forest rabble. The rich estate was engulfed in a blazing fire. Already it had eaten away the roof timbers of house and stall and barn, and the glowworms danced and howled in the glare. The looting was in full swing; they had torn open the bedding and were filling it like bags with plunder. I also saw groups stuffing themselves with provisions from the storehouses; they had smashed the lids of full barrels and were scooping out drink with their hats.

The murderers were in a gluttonous frenzy, and this worked to my advantage. I moved among them almost like a sleep-walker. Blinded by fire, by killing, and by drunkenness, they moved like creatures in a murky pond. They passed very close to me, and one, carrying a felt hat full of brandy, raised it to me with both hands before staggering off swearing when I refused to drink. I walked through them unchallenged as if the *vis calcandi supra scorpiones* were mine.

I left the wreckage of the farmstead behind, but then noticed something that made my fear grow. The intensity of the blaze behind seemed to pale—less because of the distance than because of a new and more ferocious redness that rose in the sky ahead. This section of the pasturelands was also full of commotion. I saw scattered livestock and herdsmen in flight, and above all I heard the distant baying of the red pack, which seemed to be drawing closer. I picked up my pace even as my heart filled with trepidation as I neared the terrifying ring of fire. I could already see the dark Marble Cliffs towering like black reefs in a sea of lava. And still hearing the dogs at my back, I hurriedly scaled the steep elevation from the crest of which our eyes, sublimely in-toxicated, had so often drunk in the beauty of this world now enveloped, I saw, in the purple mantle of destruction.

The extent of the devastation could be seen in the immense flames. Off in the distance, the beautiful, ancient cities on the edge of the Marina shone in their destruction. Afire, they glittered like a necklace of rubies, and their trembling reflections rose from the somber depths of the sea. All across the land, villages and hamlets burned, and flames shot up from the proud castles and the cloisters in the valleys. The smokeless flames towered like palm trees in the motionless air, raining down fire from their crowns. Flocks of pigeons and herons had risen from the reeds, and high above the swirling sparks they soared in the night's red glare. They circled until their feathers caught fire, then plunged like burning paper lanterns into the conflagration below.

Not a sound reached me, as if the entire space were devoid of air; the spectacle played out in terrible silence. I did not hear the children crying and the mothers weeping down below, nor did I hear the clansmen's battle cries or the bellowing of the cattle trapped in the stalls. Only the golden shimmer of all that horrible destruction rose to the Marble Cliffs. So distant worlds aflame delight our eyes with the beauty of their destruction.

I was also deaf to the cry that came from my own lips. Only deep within, as if I myself were engulfed in flames, did I hear the crackling of this burning world. That light crackling was all I could hear as the palaces collapsed into rubble and the sacks of grain in the warehouses by the port flew up in the air and burst into burning ash. And the large powder house at the Cock Gate exploded, rending the earth. The heavy bell that had graced the belfry for a thousand years and tolling had accompanied countless souls through life and in death glowed dimly at first, then ever brighter before finally crashing down from its beam and flattening the tower in its fall. And I saw the pediments of the pillared temples emitting red rays of light as the statues of the gods inclining with their spears and shields toppled silently into the fire.

Before this sea of fire, the dreamy stupor overcame me for a second time, and even more intensely. It is a state in which we can perceive many things at the same time, and so I heard the red pack followed by the forest rabble inexorably closing in. The dogs had almost reached the crest of the cliffs and I could hear the low bark of Chiffon Rouge as he led his howling pack. But in my stupor I was unable even to lift a foot; my scream stuck in my throat. Only once I could see the dogs was I able to move, though still under the spell. I felt I was floating down the steps of the Marble Cliffs; and then I lightly vaulted over the hedge that enclosed the garden of the Rue-Herb Retreat. Behind me the dense pack crashed past on their wild chase down the narrow cliff path.

27.

I landed half-upright in the soft ground of the lily bed and saw that the garden was marvelously illuminated. The flowers and bushes radiated a blue gleam as if they had been painted on porcelain and brought to life with a magic spell.

Lampusa and Erio stood in the kitchen courtyard above, absorbed in the sight of the conflagration. And I saw Brother Otho in his festive robe on the balcony of the retreat; he was listening in the direction of the cliff steps down which the forest rabble and the dogs were cascading like a waterfall. Soon they were swarming through the hedge like rats, and fists rattled the garden gate. Then I saw Brother Otho smile as he lifted the rock-crystal lamp and studied the small blue flame dancing in it. He hardly seemed to notice when the gate burst open under the forest rabble's blows and the dark pack, drunk with joy, trampled the lily bed, led by Chiffon Rouge with his collar of gleaming spikes.

In distress I called out to Brother Otho, who was still standing on the balcony, listening. But he did not seem to hear me for he turned without a glance and carried the lamp into the herbarium. He was acting on a higher plane—for faced with the annihilation of the work to which we had devoted our lives, he meant to consecrate it and until that was done my physical danger counted for nothing in his eyes.

I then called out to Lampusa, who was standing in the doorway of the cliff kitchen, her face lit by the fire, and when, arms crossed, she gave the teeming mass a brief glance, I saw a fierce smile bare her one tooth. I immediately knew I could expect no pity from her. As long as I got her daughter with child and slew the enemy with my sword, I was welcome; she saw every conqueror as a son-in-law, but despised any sign of weakness.

Then, when Chiffon Rouge was crouching to attack, it was Erio who came to my rescue. The boy had grabbed the silver bowl, which still stood in the courtyard after the serpent offering. He struck it, not with the pearwood spoon as he usually did, but with an iron fork. He drew from the bowl a note that sounded like a peal of laughter and froze both men and dogs in their tracks. I felt trembling coming from the fissures at the foot of the Marble Cliffs, then soft whistling, multiplied a hundredfold, filled the air. Bright flashes rent the blue light of the garden as the gleaming lancehead vipers shot out of their cracks. They slid through the flower beds like shining lashes and their undulations whipped up swirls of flower petals. Then, forming a golden circle on the ground, they slowly rose up to a man's height. Their heads swayed like heavy pendulums and their protruding fangs, ready to strike, had a deadly glint like stilettos of curved glass. Accompanying this dance, a soft hissing like hot steel being cooled in water cut through the air; and a delicate rattling like the castanets of Moorish dancers rose along the frames of the beds.

Within this ronde, the forest rabble stood petrified with fear, eyes bulging from their sockets. The Gryphon rose tallest of all; she swayed with her bright shield before Chiffon Rouge, and circled him in sinuous figures as if at play. Shuddering, its fur bristling, the monster followed the swings of the serpent's winding dance and then the Gryphon seemed barely to graze its ear. Biting its tongue in its death throes, the bloodhound writhed among the lilies.

That was the sign for the troupe of dancers who, unleashing their golden coils, flew at their prey, so thickly intertwined it seemed a single scaly body was wound around the men and the dogs. And only a single agonizing cry seemed to escape the blazing net before the poison's subtle power stifled it. Then the gleaming web unraveled and in calm undulations the serpents returned to their crevices.

All around me the flower beds lay covered with dark cadavers swollen with poison, and I looked up at Erio. I saw Lampusa leading the boy proudly and gently into the kitchen. He turned with a smile and waved at me before the gate creaked shut behind him. Now my blood coursed more easily in my veins; the spell that had stupefied me was broken. I could move my right hand freely again. Fearing for Brother Otho, I hurried into the Rue-Herb Retreat.

28.

Crossing the library, I found the books and parchments neatly arranged, the way one sets things in order before leaving on a long journey. The images of the household gods were displayed on the round table in the hall—richly provided with flowers, wine, and offerings. This room too was festively decorated and brightly illuminated by the tall candles from Sir Deodat. Ceremonious as it was, I felt at home within it. I was contemplating the adornments when Brother Otho came down from the herbarium, leaving the door to it wide open. We embraced and shared our adventures, as we used to do during lulls in battle. When I recounted how I had come upon the young prince and pulled my trophy from the leather bag, I saw Brother Otho's features harden—then, as he wept, a marvelous radiance shone from his eyes. With the wine that stood next to the offerings, we washed the head clean of blood and death sweat, then laid it in one of the large fragrant amphorae that held drying petals of white lilies and roses of Shiraz.

Then Brother Otho filled two goblets with the old wine and after pouring out libations, we drained them and smashed them on the hearth. This was our solemn farewell to the Rue-Herb Retreat, and, hearts full of sorrow, we left the house that had cloaked our spirits and our brotherhood in warmth. But turn we must from every place that shelters us on this earth.

Abandoning our possessions, we rushed through the garden gate and to the port. I held the amphora in both arms and Brother Otho hugged the mirror and the lamp safely against his chest. When we reached the curve where the path to the monastery of the Falcifera is hidden by the hills, we paused and looked back at our house. In the shadow of the Marble Cliffs, we saw its white walls and broad slate roofs that dully mirrored the shimmer of the distant fires. Terrace and balcony wrapped like dark ribbons around the light walls. So they build in those lovely valleys where, settled on the southern slopes, our people live.

As we looked back, the windows of the Rue-Herb Retreat lit up and a flame shot from the gable up to the crest of the Marble Cliffs. Its color was the same as that of the flame in Nigromontanus's lamp—a deep, dark blue—and its tip was serrated like the calyx of a gentian blossom. Thus the harvest of many years of labor fell prey to the elements and with the house, our work returned to dust. We cannot count on seeing our work completed here below, and happy is the man whose will is not too painfully invested in his efforts. No house is built, no plan created, in which ruin is not the cornerstone, and what lives imperishably in us does not reside in our works. We perceived this truth in the flame, and its glow was not devoid of joy. And so, with refreshed strength, we hurried along the path. It was still dark, but the cool of dawn already rose from the vineyard slopes and riverside pastures. In our hearts we felt that the fires in the sky were losing some of their baleful power; they were touched by the breaking dawn.

On the mountainside we saw the monastery of the Falcifera engulfed in flames. They licked at the tower, and the golden cornucopia swinging on the spindle of the weather vane was incandescent. The tall stained-glass window next to the altar with the saint's image had already shattered, and we saw Father Lampros standing in the empty room. Behind him, the room glowed like a furnace, and we rushed to the cloister's moat to call him. He was garbed in his priestly vestments and an unfamiliar smile shone on his face as if the rigidity that had always intimidated us in him had melted in the fire. He seemed to be listening and yet he did not hear our cries. Then I lifted the prince's head from the perfume amphora and raised it high in my right hand. The sight of it made us shudder, for the rose petals had soaked up the dampness of the wine and now seemed to blaze with dark purple splendor.

Yet another image captivated us when I raised the head. We saw the still-undamaged circle of the rose window in the arched frame fill with a green luster, and the rosette's pattern was oddly familiar. We had seen the same illuminated structure in the plantain Father Lampros had shown us in the monastery garden, and now this spectacle revealed the secret connection.

As I held out the head to him, the Father turned his gaze on us and slowly, half in greeting, half in demonstration, he raised his hand as in the *consecratio*, and on his finger, the large carnelian stone blazed with the light from the fire. As if he had made a sign of terrible violence with this gesture, we saw the rose window explode in a shower of golden sparks, and with the ogive, the tower and its cornucopia fell on him like a mountain.

29.

The Cock Gate had collapsed; we picked our way over the rubble. The streets were filled with the remains of walls and beams; and the corpses of the murdered lay among the debris. We saw grim scenes in the cold smoke, and yet a new confidence spread within us. Such is morning's counsel; the simple light of dawn returning after this long night seemed miraculous.

The devastation made the old disputes seem as senseless as a remembered drinking bout. Calamity alone remained. The combatants had put aside their flags and emblems. We still saw plunderers in the side streets, but the mercenaries were taking up positions in groups of two. We saw Biedenhorn posted at the Bulwark and full of self-importance. Clad in a golden cuirass but without a helmet, he stood on the square boasting that he'd already decorated the Christmas trees: he'd had his men seize whoever came along and hang them from the elm trees along the ramparts. Following military practice, he had kept himself entrenched well during the fray, but now that the entire city lay in ruins, he strutted about playing the miracle man. He was well enough informed: atop the Bulwark's round tower the Head Forester's banner with the red boar now flew.

Biederhorn was by now far gone in his cups. He was in that ferociously good mood which made him his mercenaries' favorite. He exulted that he would be free to persecute the writers, poets, and philosophers of the Marina. He detested wine and its refinement—and anything that had the scent of culture. He loved the heavy beers brewed in Britain and the Netherlands, and he looked down on the inhabitants of the Marina as snail eaters. A brawler and carouser, he firmly believed that any question on earth ought to be settled with a proper thrashing. He was like Braquemart in that— but healthier because of his contempt of theory. We appreciated his forthcoming nature and his impressive appetite. If he was out of place on the Marina, well, there's no blaming the fox that's set to guard the henhouse.

Fortunately, Biedenhorn was one those men whose memories are revived by morning drink. We did not need to remind him of the hour spent before the passes when he and his cuirassiers had gotten themselves into a tight spot. Biedenhorn had fallen from his horse there, and we saw the free peasants of the Alta Plana prying open his armor—the way a lobster's carapace, gilded by the cook's art, is cracked open at a feast. The chisel was already tickling his throat when our Purple Riders gave him and his mercenaries room to breathe. It was the very same maneuver in which the young Ansgar fell into our hands. Biedenhorn knew us from our Mauretanian days as well. So he did not stint when we asked him for a ship. Isn't the time of catastrophe the Mauretanians' finest hour? He offered us the brigantine he held in the harbor and assigned a group of his mercenaries to escort us.

The streets that lead to the harbor were thronged with refugees. Still, it seemed that not everyone wanted to leave the city: we saw the smoke of sacrifices already rising from the ruins of the temple, and the sound of chanting came from the rubble of the churches. The organ in the chapel of the Sagrada Familia, adjacent to the port, was unscathed and its powerful tones led the congregation in song:

> Princes are of women born,
> And to dust they will return;
> Their councils have been overthrown
> And now that tomb has claimed its own.
> Since no man can offer aid,
> We call on God's salvation.

Laden with their remaining belongings, people crowded into the harbor. But the ships to Burgundy and Alta Plana were already overloaded and every sailboat the dockhands pushed off with poles was followed by a wail of despair from the pier. Biedenhorn's brigantine, as if protected by a taboo, rocked on a mooring that was marked black on red and black. The ship's dark blue varnish and copper fittings gleamed, and when I gave the order to cast off, the deck boys pulled the tarpaulin covers from the red leather cushions on the benches. Because the mercenaries were holding back the crowd with their pikes, we were able to board women and children until our deck floated no more than a handsbreadth above the surface of the water. The dockhands rowed us out beyond the harbor walls. A cool wind filled our sails and pushed us towards the mountains of Alta Plana.

The freshness of dawn still lay over the water and the currents streaked its green mirroring surface. But the sun soon rose over the jagged, snowy peaks, and from the lowland haze the Marble Cliffs emerged resplendently. We looked back at them and let our hands trail in the water that in the sunlight grew blue, as if the shadows were fleeing into its depths.

We protected the amphora with great care. We were still unaware of the fate in store for this head, which we carried with us and later delivered to the Christians when they rebuilt the great cathedral on the Marina from the ruins. They would bury it beneath the foundation stone.

Before this, however, Brother Otho delivered an eburnum to the prince in the Sunmyra family seat.

30.

The men of Alta Plana had mustered at the borders when the conflagration lit up the sky. That is why we saw the young Ansgar standing on the shore before we landed; he waved at us joyfully.

We rested in the company of his men while he sent a messenger to his father, then slowly we ascended to the alpine tavern. At the passes, we lingered before the large heroon and the many smaller monuments erected in the fields there. We also came to the narrow pass from which we had extracted Biedenhorn and his mercenaries—here Ansgar gave us his hand once again and said that half of all he owned that could be shared was ours.

At noon we spotted the tavern in the old oak grove. The sight of it made us feel at home because, as in our northern country, the barns, stables, and the human residence all sheltered under one low roof. And a horse head shone from the broad gable. The gate was opened wide and the threshing floor gleamed in the sun. The livestock, their horns decorated for the day with golden ornaments, looked out over the mangers. The great hall was decorated for a feast, and from the circle of men and women waiting on the threshold, the elder Ansgar stepped forward to welcome us.

We strode through the open gate as if into the haven of our parental home.

Author's Note

I HAD ALREADY gone to bed when the car neared the vineyard with its headlights dimmed. Visits at night were, if not sinister, then certainly suspect. I asked my brother to go in my stead and returned to bed.

Through the walls I heard the conversation develop—not the words and sentences, but its increasing intensity. I got up and, in my pajamas, went to greet the guests—were there three of them or four? I have forgotten their number and their names, except for the one who was later executed. I have also forgotten what was discussed—perhaps politics were not even mentioned. But there was an odd consensus, a wordless agreement. This was the episode from which the "Sunmyra visit" developed.

It must have been a few days later when we had gathered in a small town on Lake Constance for a dinner of the local whitefish: Prince Sturdza, the composer Gerstberger, my brother, and others. Fortification of the Siegfried Line had already begun. There was a great deal of drinking; I stayed overnight in Ermatingen with the Gerstbergers. I was awakened in the morning by his singing.

I could not remember what had happened the night before even though it had been colorful; heavy drinking can bring on a kind of trance. I recalled only the beautiful lakeside cities and the flames that had been mirrored in the water. It was preliminary burning, as it is known in Westphalia and Lower Saxony.

In good humor, I strolled through the fruit orchards with the composer. Autumn was well advanced; ripe apples lay on the path. The morning sun shone on Reichenau Island. The plot had come together even down to the smallest details. It simply had to be put into words, to be recounted, which was done without haste in the spring and summer of 1939. I was already in the army when I went over the revisions.

One attendant circumstance, namely the danger of the undertaking, has been much discussed—this only marginally preoccupied me because it was tangential to the crux of the matter and too directly connected to the political foreground. That this text was provocative in that sense too was no less clear to my brother and me than it was to Paul Weinreich, the editor at the Hanseatische Verlagsanstalt, and to the publisher Benno Ziegler, for whom the publication immediately caused difficulties. It culminated in the first week with a complaint sent by Reichsleiter Bouhler to Hitler, which had no effect. I was quite well informed about all the particulars; even the harshest regime has its leaks.

In the meantime, I'd been posted to the Siegfried Line and in the bunker read reviews in domestic and foreign papers that emphasized the political aspect to a greater or lesser degree. And there was no lack of letters to the editor. "Whenever two or three of us were gathered in an idle moment, our conversations were not about the military campaign in Poland, but about this book," a student from Giessen wrote *après coup*. A few editions sold out immediately; when there were paper shortages, the army published editions under their own auspices, once in Riga and once in Paris, where it soon appeared in Henri Thomas's excellent translation.

People understood, even in occupied France, that "this shoe fit several feet." Shortly after the war there was talk of pirated editions in Ukraine and Lithuania. The only official translation on the far side of the Iron Curtain appeared in Bucharest in 1971.

So much for the political aspect. If I have made light of my friends' reproaches, I have my reasons. Although this assault from the realm of dreams reflects and captures the nightmarish political situation, it also transcends—in time and space—the scope of the actual and the episodic.

To this was added a growing allergy to the word "resistance." A man can harmonize with the powers of his time or he can stand against them. This is secondary. At every point he has the opportunity to show how he has grown. That is how he can manifest his freedom—physical, spiritual, moral—especially in the face of danger. How will he remain true to himself: that is his problem. It is also the touchstone of the poem.

December 10, 1972

AFTERWORD

THE IMPORTANCE of Ernst Jünger and the interest of his most recent book, *On the Marble Cliffs,* charge critics with the duty of not letting this work be lost among the general run of translations set before them. In fact, we have to consider the work of Jünger, still a young writer, as one of the most remarkable of our time. It has a violence of meaning and an artistic power that often make it exemplary. One wishes that the young French novelists could learn to know and see in it, as in the masterpieces of contemporary American and English literature, what an art aware of its laws can achieve in the novelistic genre.

According to a few commentators, *On the Marble Cliffs* is not a novel. That is a question of pure form. The book, which is short (150 pages in the German edition), is a narrative whose entire structure expresses the work of the imagination. It portrays strongly depicted characters and constitutes a story that takes place according to clearly defined series of events. A horizon of mountain, forest, and city serves as a backdrop for it, and one can read it without seeing anything besides the tragic and poetic details that give it such reality. What could it lack to be a real novel? Nothing at all. If someone wants to categorize it under other genres, it is because the book offers this originality of offering a meaning. It leaves the impression of calling into question not only men but forces, and it abandons the reader to a strange intellectual atmosphere. A novel that, under pretext of actual adventures, draws the intelligence into a symbolic labyrinth—that is what confronts the ways of a tradition more conventional than rigorous and always uneasy about forms that it can't recognize.

On the surface it is easy enough to summarize a story that develops in a few simple episodes. In reality the movement of the fiction is so subtly manipulated that any analysis troubles its perspective. Charm and intention are lost in it. It is in an imaginary country, enriched with a few allusions to real countries, that the two witnesses of the drama come to live. This region has a mysterious magnificence that comes from perfectly described and yet elusive beauties, as a land of enigmas might be. From the summit of the hermitage where they have retired to pursue the study of plants, the two solitary figures see the territory of the Marina stretch out, a rich plain of vineyards, inhabited by a peaceful and happy population, separated from great forests by a long stretch of fields and marshes. Beyond the sea, dotted with islands, the summits of the Alta Plana sparkle. In this country an ancient civilization still shines where, according to the regions, the traits of a primitive Christianity or the customs of old pagan traditions are visible. Between the Marina plain, whose rich fertility has allowed the elaboration of an almost perfect work of culture, and the obscure tribes of the high forests that the Oberförster, the Head Forester, leads, the threat of a decisive struggle causes grave forebodings. The two hermits, isolated by their labors and their retreat, see clouds pile up over the old world. The Head Forester, with the outlaws to whom he grants asylum, with his sinister mob of demons and lemures, exercises a tyrannical oppression on the population of shepherds. Disorder reaches the city. The Oberförster has allies or accomplices everywhere. He provokes agitations that he himself represses. He spreads anarchy while playing the role of a force for order. He has in his pay the magistrates who are supposed to prosecute his crimes, as well as the hired soldiers supposed to eliminate the danger. The old world yields to its decline in the indifference of half sleep.

When the struggle breaks out openly, the two hermits, although they know the weakness of this civilization fated to ruin, are too attached to its profound treasures not to try to defend them, so they do not remain aloof. They have received a visit from the Prince of Sunmyra and from Braquemart, both representatives and guardians of the ancient culture, one by his nobility that old blood already relegates to the world of the dead, the other as theoretician of violence, readier to find a nihilistic ideal to his taste than to find concrete methods to fight unrestrained anarchy. These last representatives of a vanished power go to provoke the Head Forester in his domain, and the Forester, leading his lugubrious bands, surrounded by dogs whom he has trained for carnage, leaves the woods and drives his conquest through villages and towns, where the great wealth slowly accumulated in them is lost in the collapse of an entire world. While a conflagration consumes peace, happiness, perfection, the two solitaries, after having sacrificed the fruits of their labor to the fire of a magic mirror, reach the open sea, carrying with them, last vestige of this annihilated culture, the head of the noble Prince of Sunmyra, murdered by the barbarian legions.

We must immediately be discouraged from recognizing in this story the characteristics of a simplistic allegorical interpretation. That is when Ernst Jünger's originality is revealed. In the field of the imagination, where everything seems prepared for the symbolic, where the main features of the narrative are charged with a clearly expressed significance, where brief abstract meditations are interwoven, the figures bathed in strange intellectual light finally escape the mind that tries to grasp them and interpret them according to its laws. The world that it illustrates does not answer to the one that we are used to contemplating; the men who move in it do not have the natural life that makes any symbolic significance irrelevant to them, and in fact the reality whose expression it conveys is also entirely different from the one that intelligence can conceive. It is a matter of a universe that, although in some aspects intellectual, is nonetheless as remote from the world of the mind as the world of banal truth can be from it. We could perhaps form an idea of it by imagining a fiction that would be to the life of our mind what dream is to reality of the previous day. Our intelligence too has a dream in which notions, definitions, ordered meditations no longer have the meaning that the laws of day give them. Thought dreams of things and of itself in a mirror in which images represent it as it is in its cold sleep. It abandons itself to a gaze that juxtaposes its significance onto a thing and onto this significance a new reality that is like the prolonging of it into nothingness. The beyond of the mind is symbolized by this world that is open to us.

It is to such a transposition that Jünger's art keeps leading us, one that gives it its lofty singularity. The drama of the Marina unfolds in a region where we could say that everything is symbol but where the symbol itself is broken as figure and needs to be replaced by the changing images that reflect the other side of the horizon. The plants whose eternal laws the hermits investigate, the venomous snakes that live in the path near the hermitage in easy familiarity with the hosts who feed them, the mirror of the magician Nigromontanus in which the treasures burned by flames survive in spirit, beyond destruction, in the nothingness that it has procured for them—all these figures who tend to translate themselves into clearly defined notions finally banish the thought that they summoned and construct outside of it an order that needs no other reason for being.

It is the same with the story that takes place in the imaginary country. We could perhaps try to find what tendency the images that occur in it indicate. But the proof that the story does not depend on an interpretation that would reveal it is that this interpretation would only repeat the story itself and does not dissipate the atmosphere of violence and tragic strangeness. It is quite obvious that the Head Forester's struggle against the happy and peaceful Marina represents one of those moments of crisis of human history in which the work of civilization is threatened by absolute oppression. This cruel and robust old man hates the plow and domestic labor. He hates the work of poets and the place that shelters it. He uses all perverse forces and reigns in the heart of forests, in a harsh environment where a light shines that is not that of the sun. Against this power, who obviously symbolizes demoniac and elementary forces, the narrator takes sides with a lofty calm sadness hardly equaled except in Goethe. If the old world appears in the already compromised sovereignty that the temptation of decline brings it, if its defenders are themselves devoted to their end by the excess of what they are, the Prince of Sunmyra too noble, too old in his youth, Braquemart too intelligent to save intelligence, it is nonetheless not as heroes of a condemned era that they die but as witnesses to a truth that is threatened along with them and that like them is at risk of perishing. Father Lampros, last branch of the religious tree, drops from the height of his altar a supreme benediction on the head of the unfortunate martyr prince, and this head itself, enclosed in a precious amphora, among the flowers and perfumes, escapes destruction, symbol of what can always be saved in a civilization that is disappearing, image of the mind that survives works and on which the future is based. "We protected the amphora with great care," says the narrator. "We were still unaware of the fate in store for this head, which we carried with us and later delivered to the Christians when they rebuilt the great cathedral on the Marina from the ruins. They would bury it beneath the foundation stone."

It would be absurd, even on the level of intellectual fiction, to regard this first approximation of *On the Marble Cliffs* as an explanation that exhausts its themes. The movement that makes this book into the tragedy of the creative mind witnessing its ruin with a serene anguish endlessly deepens the vision. What rises up beneath our gaze is a world where everything that is precious seems already caught in destruction, where barbaric force necessarily breaks the forms of the finest thought, and where nonetheless this nothingness into which the mind sinks allows something to survive, like its truest emanation, that neither metamorphoses nor death can corrupt. The admirable myth of Nigromontanus participates in this proud hope for annihilation. Legacy of an old master versed in magic, this mirror has the property of concentrating rays of light on things of such a brightness that they are consumed in it by regaining the eternal, and are preserved in it in the domain of the invisible. "Things set alight by such heat became imperishable in a way Nigromontanus said could best be compared to pure distillation . . . [He] called it security in the void." Similarly for Father Lampros there is nothing terrifying about destruction, for he is one of those natures born to penetrate into the exalted flames as one enters the gate into one's ancestral home. And, adds the narrator, "Father Lampros, living like a dreamer behind the monastery walls, was perhaps the only one of us to live at the heart of reality." Thus Jünger's book reflects, in the anguish of general collapse, the temptation of fire where the spirit saves, by losing it, that which is essential to it, and is delivered by this very ruin from the oppressive hope for salvation.

Ernst Jünger's style is very beautiful. Of a slow, almost formal allure, enclosing the lofty revelation of a message in phrases that never give way to vulgar ease, it offers words all the force that careful choice shaped to their inner and outer truth, to their reality and to their appearances, to the primordial sounds whose source they conserve. Language, in this calculated art, is an appeal to powers that knowledge cannot discover; and like a weapon forged in fire, it has the admirable coldness, the cruel dignity that makes the object richest in memories into the most effective instrument.

—Maurice Blanchot

1943
Translated by Charlotte Mandell

OTHER NEW YORK REVIEW CLASSICS

For a complete list of titles, visit www.nyrb.com.